MATE

a novel in twenty games

Robert Castle

SPUYTEN DUYVIL
New York City

Library of Congress Control Number: 2025932284

The Pillsbury-Larkin Match is a hypermodern game, whence control becomes the real necessity in a marriage. These grandmasters had studied the games that their parents had played and refused to play by the classic rules and general principles. In other words, love would be relegated to the background, inappropriate for the type of struggles and ends of behavior manifested by wholehearted faith in flanking moves. What gains importance throughout the match is each player's dependence on deft psychological moves (for example, imitating the other player's moves, in a sense showing that every move has its opposite reaction). Another aspect of the "flanking game" in Pillsbury-Larkin is manifested in the brilliant opening moves.

As per all matches *à propos* marriage, the number of games played is open. The death of both spouses has in many cases failed to terminate a match. Since spectators demand a winner in every marriage skirmish, the first player to reach six wins wins. Seemingly inconsequential moves can determine the victor. Psychological brutality alone would have satisfied the patrons of the Roman Colosseum.

In this Marriage-Games textbook, the editors present seven games with clear outcomes, two draws (one of which many contemporary commentators suggest had really decided the match), and one of the few stalemates at the Championship level of competition.

The Baby Exploit

This first match between these Masters might be the most memorable. Flawlessly played by Larkin, Game 1 establishes her effectiveness as Black. One cannot help admiring Pillsbury's moves once his defeat had become inevitable to him.

Pillsbury: *White*   Larkin: *Black*

1. (*White*) Pillsbury is about to leave her apartment an hour after they have sex.

1. (*Black*) "Do you think we'll ever get married?" asks Cynthia.

2. (*White*) "I always figured we would get married," Bill smiles.

Technically bad. Better: **2. Gets on his knees** and 3. **"Will you marry me?"** White forces Black to listen but restricts her own development. The seeming inconvenience of the slow start will be amply rewarded by a strong endgame. Remember: KEEP HER HAPPY is one of his goals of the early games in this match. A player such as Pillsbury often forgets that yielding to one's opponent can lead to rewarding, even winning developments. 2. **"I figured we would get married"** might have been suitable for another

match, or if Black *had opened* with "**I think I'm pregnant.**"
Black had really been reserving that decisive move for
later, for when the couple might *still* be unengaged.

2. (*Black*) Retains her maiden name after the wedding.

3. (*White*) "I don't even wear a watch," he says when he
declines to wear a wedding ring.
3. (*Black*) She goes to Mass every Sunday and takes
communion.

4. (*White*) He attends Midnight Mass on Christmas with
his parents, brothers, sisters, nephews, and nieces; Easter
Mass with his wife and in-laws, to fulfill the yearly
obligations.
4. (*Black*) "Where are the car keys, honey?"

Black's move makes her opponent believe she is scratching
around for a Plan. It will not be the last time Pillsbury will
underestimate Larkin – indeed, the next underestimation
will be in overestimating her capabilities, i.e., believing
she has a Plan when in fact she's scratching around for
one.

5. (*White*) "I don't know. I never drive your car."

White sees little prospect in helping her out. An
alternative: **5. "Not again!"** would be too harsh. Berating

one's opponent has to be sustained for an entire game, and Pillsbury knows that he does not pack that weapon. Even so, the game would have been livelier if White had taken such a verbal shot from nowhere. Nothing provokes more anxiety than the mixture of verbal violence followed by news of a pregnancy. The later games will see little of such good judgment.

5. (*Black*) She insists they food shop together despite the couple's previous rancorous behavior when he suggested the last thing she needed was ice cream.

He does not see the strategic value of asking why she thinks she needs ice cream. And he does not see the aggressiveness of asking rhetorical questions. **Game 17** will give the interested spectator an insight into the symbolic importance of shopping together. When one or the other players shops alone, the seeds of discontent are sown, watered, and blooming simultaneously.

6. (*White*) "Let's get lamb chops for tonight."
6. (*Black*) "We can't afford them; we're having meat loaf."

7. (*White*) "What do you mean we can't afford lamb chops?"

Tit-for-tat. He astutely interpreted her remark as a deprecation of his low-paying job. Nothing unusual here. Perhaps he learned from an earlier match between his parents, Pillsbury - Hutton, when his father responded to a similar move to take food from his table: "**A man works and expects roast beef or tenderloin, not flank steak.**" White's "**What do you mean...?** response also ensures that no feelings will be spared and that a **Draw** is now unlikely.

7. (*Black*) "I'll meet you in the car," and she hands him the half-full brown plastic basket.

8. (*White*) First Anniversary:
    a. sends serious romantic card
    b. buys dinner ($58.80)
    c. no flowers

Some experts might blame his **8c** move for the weakness of this move. Others who follow the games of these opponents will tell you that **8c. Oral sex with a flower stuck up her ass at orgasm** would not have sufficed. Could he still be paying for **2. "I always figured we'd get married"**?

8. (*Black*) Second Anniversary:
    a. She sends funny card
    b. Buys him a sweater (on their joint-charge)
    c. Insists on eating at home

9. (*White*) Joins a Fantasy Football League. He calls his team The Terminators.

9. (*Black*) "I should be able to fit into a size eight by next week."

Male bonding threat met by a king-side attack: Larkin's two sizes reduction was noticed by other men. Her husband, Bill, was not unaware of *Black*'s fervent desire for his next move to be **10. Will not have his friends over on Sundays to watch the games.** This move is unlikely for many reasons. The league's rules state that each fantasy general manager will host other general managers once during the season and, possibly, again if his team made the playoffs. Secondly, the way he would actually make this particular move would have had a modicum of self-effacement: **10. "Cynth, I lucked out, I don't have to host this week,"** although not necessarily depriving *Black* the warm triumph of having avoided inevitable disaster, as was coming in the next move.

10. (*White*) "I'll pay for it," says Tom Gentry, one Sunday during football season after breaking one of Bill's wedding presents, a vase, in the shape of a boot, white with pink flowers down the sides because her Aunt Rita, who had a tendency to visit unannounced, had given it to them.
10. (*Black*) "When we have children, do you think we'll be able to afford the dues for this league?"

11. (*White*) Watches television, rapidly changing channels with the remote.

White declines *Black*'s gambit. If he had responded: **11. "It doesn't cost that much,"** Pillsbury would have missed the real meaning of **10. "When we have children. . . ."** Likewise, he would have engendered: **11. . . "I've been doing some calculating on my own,"** from Larkin, and he would have had to counter: **12. "I was actually thinking of joining a Baseball Rotisserie League this summer."** All this maneuvering would then have been for nothing. *Black*'s **10. "When we have children..."** move had nothing to do with the FFL or other vicarious outlets for Bill's boredom. Larkin simply dislikes his friends, broken ugly vase or not. White's oblique "channel surfing" response, delightfully indulging in its own misdirection, deserves analysis. Bill had always annoyed Cynthia with this habit (her habit was of a more covert nature, jumping from two or three shows, all of which Bill despised). To raise such incidental behavior to the level of "a move" reminding Larkin what a true instrument of terror her husband could wield in this match. White would have had tougher time with **10... She expects Aunt Rita to leave them something substantial in her will.** Likewise, *she* would have had a tougher time had *White* moved **9. Buys foose ball table**, because his friends would be coming over on days of the week other than Sundays, Bill's monetary investment in the table would be more substantial than ten seasons in fantasy football, and, most importantly, they had no room in their apartment for such a table. Thus, *Black*'s **9... "Where do we have room to put the** table?" would have been effectively countered with **10. "I didn't even think about that!"** Such blissful ignorance by the male player in the marriage game has often been called the "cart before the horse" move. The female player historically has molded her game to deal with a husband's pitiful ignorance.

11. (*Black*) Refuses to program the VCR. (!)

She knows how but claims not to. He knows she knows how. An inability to handle new technical hardware by Cynthia's mother had worn down Larkin in Larkin – Walsh in the 1960s.

12. (*White*) Programs her favorite television shows when they go out on Saturday night.
12. (*Black*) Watches her recorded programs when he would rather watch his own favorite shows – and now he can't even record those.

13. (*White*) "You haven't looked at all well the last few days."
13. (*Black*) "I made an appointment to see Doctor Pearlman."

Black expects: **14. Bill will take off from work to drive her to the doctor's office.** This would have been the safe move for Pillsbury.

14. (*White*) "Do you think you're pregnant?"   (?)

White's mistake was now written on his face. Not that he doesn't want children. Just not this soon. And it was this latter flinch that *Black* detected in his tremulous question. Really, he was happy. Too late now!!! Cynthia thinks (or worse: she thinks she thinks) that he thought that now he could not afford joining a Baseball Rotisserie League. Infinitely better for Pillsbury: **14. Smiles and kisses**, or (a winning combination in some games) **14. Takes her to bed**. Pillsbury - Hutton followed the latter, whereas the former was observed in Larkin - Walsh. To indicate generational difference, many of Bill's married friends (Clifton-Chalmers; Phillips-Zimmerman) opted for **I want a boy (or girl)** and **He is happy to know that he's not sterile**.

14. (*Black*) "Let's not tell anyone right away."

Which meant: **I'll tell my mother while we keep yours in the dark**. In-laws will figure more severely in later games.

15. (*White*) Tells his buddies at the landscaping business that he is going to be a daddy.

The crude logic of this move can only be understood in light of *White*'s previous blunder. Pillsbury is of the school that the only way to recover from a mistake is to take the offensive and allow his lack of repentance to achieve victory blindly. Indeed, his apparent reluctance to have a child (I emphasize "apparent") contrasts with later near obsession to have a second child, except that the future obsession was motivated less by wanting a child than for a way to save his marriage. Perhaps not wanting a child and doing his best to deprive Cynthia from having children would have been his best game plan for the entire Match. Of course, this assumes that Cynthia was happy to have her first pregnancy, that is, happy with the timing, so early in their marriage.

15. (*Black*) Takes him to the shopping center for the ostensible purpose of buying porch furniture; suddenly, they find themselves amidst diapering tables (on sale).

16. (*White*) "We don't need a diapering table," he says firmly.
16. (*Black*) "How are we going to change the kid?"

An apparently senseless exchange (moreover, a public one!), unless one (like Larkin) *interprets* Pillsbury's move **16.** as really saying **"Why the hell are we having children?"** And if Pillsbury actually meant this, he should have said it! Was having a child going to hold him back (professionally!)? Or perhaps he felt the world did not need another voracious American mouth to feed? From Larkin's perspective, her husband was refusing to accept her enceint condition.

17. (*White*) "On the bed or a chair," he answers.

White continues this nonsensical verbal exchange only because he sees the possibility of a retreat by *Black*, a possibility she will not let happen.

17. (*Black*) "They aren't expensive," she replies loudly, as other customers in the store glance uneasily at this young couple.

18. (*White*) "What did people use eighty or hundred years ago? I don't know anyone who has one."
18. (*Black*) "What the hell are you talking about, you asshole?" she cries out and starts sobbing.

19. (*White*) Takes her to the parking lot, cursing her for making them look like fucking fools.
19. (*Black*) Silent as they drive home

In an ideological resumption of moves **5 to 7**, this furious flurry finds *White* progressively cornering himself after the wrong turn at **14**.

20. (*White*) "Why aren't we going home?" Cynthia asks him, responding to his taking a u-turn.

Not for nothing do the manuals say that one should never take back a move. Yes, Bill was looking for a store which sold diapering tables. Why not return to the Ikea? The choice between appearing to have made an error and acknowledging an error could, and would in a later game, mark the difference between losing and not losing, but not necessarily winning. In a later interview, he admitted the error in move **20** while stating that it seemed the best way to handle *Black* at the time. He might have considered **20. Submits the following names for the expectant child: Winchester, Zephyr, Demeter, Lattimore, Dortmunder, Clea.** In a grander strategy, *White* must maintain a stance at once unapologetic for his **14. "Do you think you're pregnant?"** sentiment but not too removed from the birthing process. He could then have followed the naming with **21. Volunteer his mother to take care of the child**, more than hinting that he would want Cynthia to get back to her job teaching English at a private school as quickly as possible. However, Cynthia knows her opponent too well and seems one step ahead of him the remainder of the game. Many of her best moves come when *White* tries too hard to make up for his errors.

20. (*Black*) Volunteers *her mother* to take care of the child so that she can get back to school.

21. (*White*) Watches the World Skating Championships.

This and upcoming moves might have had the appearance of strength *if* they had come before move **20**. Now they seem only pathetic. Also, "**Watches Ice Skating**" would have had more power if Cynthia had not been home. And then telling her what she had missed! Even better: **21. Tells her he watched the World Skating Championships but really had not.** Nor would her response: **21. She doesn't believe him** have worked, because he would have established that he would lie to her shamelessly at any time. From that point he might have been able to keep her in constant check with lies and half-truths.

21. (*Black*) She buys the book *Women Who Love Too Much*.

22. (*White*) Listens to the baby move in her stomach every evening.

22. (*Black*) "Wouldn't it be great if we had twins?" she comments after a visit to the doctor's office.

23. (*White*) Starts going to Church on Sunday.

This move loses amusingly.

23. (*Black*) Stops going to Church, explaining that her condition is making her feel faint when sitting in a pew surrounded by the crowd.

Black knows that *White* dares not take back move **23**, a move, by the way, which begs for disdain given *Black's* move **22**. If **24. Tells her he went to Church but actually did not** (cf. commentary above after move **21**), *Black* replies **24...She has no response**, or **Asks him what priest served Mass**. If **25. "Father Constantine"**, who married them, her triumph will only be delayed when she **25... Drops the matter**, or be sped up when **25...She has called the Church beforehand to see who had served the Mass**. Does *White* want to go through this agony? All it will accomplish is an attrition of forces which will never see him catching up.

24. (*White*) "We should move out of this apartment and find a bigger place."

Much better: **24. "There was a burglary in the downstairs apartment,"** but the reason for this move is hard for *White* to see.

24. (*Black*) "I like this area. There are a bunch of beginning families in the neighborhood."

25. (*White*) "Wouldn't you like it better near Princeton?"
25. (*Black*) "Most of my friends live around here."

26. (*White*) Gets drunk at his company's Christmas party.
26. (*Black*) "I can't believe you drove home in that condition."

Black's instincts had been preparing for **26. . ."Who were you flirting with this year?"**

27. (*White*) Works extra hours to build up the bank account.

The failure of previous moves to reverse an unfavorable trend has led to this: ostensibly saving for the expectant child's college education. Pillsbury has settled into a routine which keeps him away from the apartment more than ever and, in a way, justifies her possibly saying **26...** **"Who were you flirting with?"** Yet, had *White* spent more time with his opponent, would this have been enough to wrest the victory from her?

27. (*Black*) "You were probably hoping I wanted an abortion."

28. (*White*) Quits his FFL and decides not to join the Baseball Rotisserie League.

A desperate attempt to breathe. Foreshadows his ultimate resignation.

28. (*Black*) "What if the doctors says the kid's deformed or retarded? Do you think you'll be able to find it in yourself to love the baby?"

29. (*White*) RESIGNS

An excellent example of a one-way tactical battle, although it is atypical of the games in the Pillsbury-Larkin match. One wonders how much Pillsbury was shaken by his loss in this game. The tactical advantage was lost less than a year into his marriage, and, given the nature of the next game, his cause would appear to be doomed thereafter.

MATCH SCORE: Pillsbury 0 – Larkin 1

NOTE:

Marriage players and theoreticians have long debated whether, given perfect play by both sides, the game should end in a win or a draw. Since World War II, when these games became popular, the consensus has been that perfectly played games should end in a draw. A few vocal group players and commentators have maintained that there never can really be a winner. It can only be that one person loses. Others have argued that White's advantage may have been sufficient to force a win, claiming that White was winning after the first move. Unless that move was reckless, mostly a matter of the player's temperament, that is, the player, usually the man, is an incorrigible asshole. Fears have been expressed that a "draw death" is more likely as the Marriage games are more deeply analyzed and the players more psychologically informed. To alleviate this danger, I, among others, have suggested changing how draws and stalemates are scored. Some analysts have challenged the view that White has an inherent advantage, and there have been a series of books on the theme that "Black is OK!", arguing that the perception that White has an advantage is founded more in psychology than reality, and that White's advantage *qua* White disappears for no apparent reason as a game progresses. Finally, it has been suggested that Black has certain countervailing advantages. The consensus that White should try to win can be a psychological burden for the White player, who sometimes" trying too hard to live up to his supposedly inherent advantage. Symmetrical openings (i.e. those where Black's moves mirror White's) can lead to situations where moving first is a detriment, for either psychological or objective reasons.

Cute Baby Game

Few interested in the play of Masters have found much to say about the follow-up to one of the more interesting games in the Match. Called the Cute Baby game because of an offhand remark that resulted in the only excitement. Experts on Pillsbury - Larkin, however, say that close study of this game explains much about the overall outcome of the Match.

Larkin:	*White*		Pillsbury:	*Black*

1. (*White*) "Do you want a boy or a girl?"

An opening as powerful, and as stultifying, as marking an X in the center square of tic-tac-toe. All subsequent moves being equal (among the Marriage Masters), the result should be nothing less than a draw for *White*. Larkin's choice of opening surely was dictated by her victory in **Game One**. The pressure on Pillsbury would be tremendous. Other similar moves include 1. **"You wouldn't mind much if we had a girl"** and 1. **"Do you think we should have waited longer before having a child?"** The latter traditionally has gotten some winning results. She is a great master, using her biology to maximum psychological advantage. Imagine a man attempting to use his own passive libidinal traits to argue *anything*.

1. (*Black*) "Little girls are just as precious as little boys."

All moves being equal, although they never are, this should guarantee no less than a draw. The equivalent to putting an O in one of the corner squares to stop a centered X every time. *Black* has decided not to put up a fight until the kid is born.

2. (*White*) "Do you want to know if it will be a boy or a girl?
2. (*Black*) "Only if you do."

More of the same from *Black*. He is trying to stay on his feet after sustaining some well-placed blows in the previous game. Better, he should examine the potential gain to himself by being less diffident.

3. (*White*) Cynthia works until one week before giving birth.
3. (*Black*) Bill tells his in-laws that he'd have preferred Cynthia to stay home and take care of the child until it went to school. "Kids are going to school earlier and earlier," he offers pointlessly.

4. (*White*) She informs her in-laws that Bill should request sick leave from his job the first month she's home from the hospital. "This will be the most important time in our child's life."

4. (*Black*) He was in the hospital but not present for the birth of his daughter.

5. (*White*) "Where *were* you, Bill? I've never suffered worse pain."

Very effective move to couple the question with her pain, suggesting that the pain would have been very much eased by his presence. Nor could Bill have dared to say: **5... "When did my being around ever make your pain go away?"** He had to be satisfied with a weaker excuse.

5. (*Black*) "I only went out to get a cup of coffee. You were in labor so long I thought...."

6. (*White*) "But for our first child...."
6. (*Black*) "We'll have more opportunities, babe."

What strikes this observer more sharply: the nonchalance of his "babe" or the utterly preposterous sincerity of the words coming from the lips of a man who knew they could not afford more kids?

7. (*White*) Her version: they had decided on 'Emily' for a girl and 'Lawrence' for a boy.
7. (*Black*) His: 'Lenore' and 'John Patrick.'

8. (*White*) To be named after the poet...well, every student

in Cynthia's English classes could have told you what the name of her daughter-to-be would be!

8. (*Black*) He likes the sound of Lenore and has no reason for choosing it save that it sounds noble.

9. (*White*) Could she disappoint the 50 or so students who so much enjoyed studying those short poems?

9. (*Black*) What about a compromise? Name the baby after Cynthia. He thought of them as one.

An attempt to win the match with bald flattery. Its obviousness is what makes it so sly. Yet this move has been tried in previous matches. Pillsbury-Hutton had lasted 89 moves before Bill's father named him but still did not carry the game to victory. Why? A male child creates an advantage for the father only for several moves until the father realizes the kid always wants his mother. Thus, a male player may stupidly insist on naming the child after himself or, worse, will manufacture a name (see commentary after move **20** in **Game One** above) that would cause untold damage to the child. The rule generally applies only to the first child born in the marriage. Besides, the woman loses automatically if she assents to naming the boy after the father with roman numerals. Better for *Black*: **9... Suggests a boy's name for their daughter.**

10. (*White*) "Emily," Cynthia said as her daughter first

suckled at her breast.

Larkin's decisive strength in many of her battles with Pillsbury can best be seen in her simplest moves.

10. (*Black*) Bill suggests that Larry Phillips, his friend for five years in the landscaping business, be the godfather.

11. (*White*) Her cousin Jeanne is the godmother, they were like sisters growing up; Bill's brother, Peter, became the godfather after she pressed Bill to name a second choice. 11. (*Black*) Larry and he are thinking of starting their own landscaping business.

Black doesn't want to admit to losing the advantage. The only means of retribution is to persist with the argument long after the naming ritual has been settled. Why? He wants to plant a seed and, should it not help this game, certainly he will benefit in a later game when work, money, and a good life become the issues. Her choice of godfather had effectively deprived them of income which would have given them a better house more quickly, more time to have fun together, and proper gratification of their children's consumer demands. In effect, he will have convinced her that their future divorce was her fault. It will become one of many similar strategies to get Cynthia to feel this way. Who knows: this may be the single move that will have allowed Bill to win the entire match!

12. (*White*) "Your family completely ignored my mother and aunt at the party after the christening."

12. (*Black*) "My sister, Judy, talked to them."

13. (*White*) "She was the only one."

13. (*Black*) "And your Aunt Rita bent my mom's ear about not being invited to my cousin's wedding."

14. (*White*) "She thought she should have been."

Better: **14. "We invited *your* cousin to our wedding."** However, there was nothing *White* could do about the following jabs (accomplished in one move) from *Black*.

14. (*Black*) "She doesn't know her, for God's sake. Besides, didn't you tell me that she was working that weekend?"

15. (*White*) "She could always get off."

15. (*Black*) "You said she was glad she wasn't invited."

16. (*White*) Cynthia returns to work a week after the christening.

Not: **16. "I was just saying that."** The order of Larkin's moves is more than academic. *White* knows how to dovetail a losing group of moves back to a (previous) winning combination.

16. (*Black*) Wasn't her school paying full benefits until the end of the semester?

17. (*White*) "As yearbook moderator, I have to be there to keep the students on the right track."
17. (*Black*) "You could have saddled someone else with it."

Black's error: assuming the logical move (the logical thing to say) was the logical move.

18. (*White*). Yearbook pays an extra $1500 a year.

White's error: Thinking he would both absorb *and* forget the inference to her making more money per year than he makes.

18. (*Black*) Bill's mother took care of Emily twice a week, Tuesday and Wednesdays, saving the Pillsburys $150 per week on Daycare costs.

19. (*White*) Mrs. Larkin would have gladly taken care of Emily on one or two other days, had she been asked.

What one might interpret as a weak response contains a particle of strength. Cynthia didn't want her mother to take care of the child. Although she believed Emily should see her grandmother, and vice versa, the mere thought of seeing her mother gave Cynthia high blood pressure. Her volunteering her mother for childcare duty was a clear feint by Cynthia to insure less friction between herself and her mother. In Larkin - Walsh, Cynthia's mother moved to keep her husband's family away from her house, especially on weekdays, by paying Rita, her sister, twenty-five dollars for three-afternoons of work when Mrs. Larkin took a part-time job at Macy's.

19. (*Black*) He drives Emily to the daycare center on the way to work.

20. (*White*) She picks up Emily in the afternoon on the way home from teaching.
20. (*Black*) Bill changes Emily's diapers two or three times daily.

21. (*White*) Cynthia remarks that he only handles the shit-free Pampers.
21. (*Black*) "That's not true."

22. (*White*) "Are you still attracted to me?"
22. (*Black*) Throws a shitty diaper into the kitchen trash bucket that their dachshund, Bart, later tears in ten pieces, carrying several to the couple's bedroom.

Not: **22. "Why would you say that?"** Prompting *White*'s response **23. "You haven't touched me in months.** Followed by the disastrous *Black* **23...We've both been** too tired to…" Disastrous partly because he did not finish the sentence.

23. (*White*) "I told you to always throw them in the outside trash."
23. (*Black*) He was going to do that later but forgot.

Insisting that he handle shitty diapers may have been an error in judgment on Cynthia's part, but not enough to give him an advantage. Some commentators believe *Black*'s apparent misstep was the result of move **22. "Are you still attracted to me?"** Such questions by wives cannot be ignored. Others say that his **22…Throws a shitty….** was the best way to handle it because it gave *White* the impression that the move had greater importance than it really had, whereas Bart the dog was the real winner.

24. (*White*) "You know how Bart gets into everything we put in there."
24. (*Black*) Bart becomes susceptible to epileptic seizures and must be taken to an emergency veterinary ward.

Black is not beyond accepting help for his game from the canine brigade. The dachshund's poor physiology deflates *White*'s gambit to make her husband feel really stupid. However, she must follow through, as did Philip II with the Armada to England.

25. (*White*) Maybe if Bill thought....

Complete the thought! Complete the thought! It is not enough to control or occupy space – you must be able to retain it. She cannot let *Black* outmaneuver her by making the move she was going to make. By posing the following tough questions, *Black* put *White* on the defensive.

25. (*Black*) Offhandedly, he wonders whether they should get rid of Bart.

26. (*White*) "I hear Emily crying," she says at three o'clock in the morning.
26. (*Black*) Bill checks in Emily's room and finds the baby sleeping.

27. (*White*) "I hear Emily crying," she says four days later around the same time.
27. (*Black*) "Check for yourself."

28. (*White*) Brings back the crying infant.
28. (*Black*) "What's wrong with her."

It would have been a big mistake for him to say: **28...."Did you wake her up to prove you heard her?"**

29. (*White*) Cynthia asks Bill whom he thinks the baby looks like.

29. (*Black*) "I don't know."

30. (*White*) Mrs. Larkin had said that Emily looked like Mr. Larkin.

30. (*Black*) Bill had never met Cynthia's father, who died fifteen years ago when Cynthia was twelve.

Just when you think it safe. A move like *Black*'s here – a move handed to him by fate – should have led to an amicable draw. Little did he know how much work it would take to get that Draw.

31 (*White*) Her mother has never been "right" since Mr. Larkin died.

A lesson from the Marriage Matches. Yes, Mr. Larkin died a while ago but the dead Mr. Larkin continued in Mrs. Larkin's mind. And still continues. Moves from a dead man are hard to defend.

31. (*Black*) Bill remarks absently that Emily's ears stick out.

32. (*White*) Cynthia tearfully runs into the bedroom and locks the door.

For *Black* to counter with **32...**"**What did I say?**" would have been woefully inadequate here. Restraint is a method of insuring spatial advantage by preventing moves which would permit *White* to expand her indignation. It appears that Bill's deep strategy is to so consistently bollox things up that Cynthia can't not win. It would be naïve to think that Bill actually intends this.

32. (*Black*) He immediately follows and knocks on the door asking her to come out.

The reparation process begins quickly, quietly, effectively. **32. Leaves the house** and **33. Goes to a bar** or **33. Goes to his mother's** might have been sufficient to deal with the matter, showing *White* that she was overreacting and that he has better things to do than to wet nurse his wife.

33. (*White*) "Go to hell you motherfucking shit."

White's response indicates that complying with his salutations would not be useful here. The move is not bad, merely unnecessary. **"Go to hell you motherfucking shit,"** as a move, only gives the player satisfaction and does nothing for developing control of the marriage board.

33. (*Black*) "Not until we talk."

Humor doesn't hurt in this situation. Bill's flexibility in an apparent crisis, besides showing a modicum of compassion, even false compassion, usually is not a trait exhibited by those in the landscaping trade. Equally important, he must ignore *White*'s moves until he sees a chance to better his position. Getting him to react to her emotion is what she really wants.

34. (*White*) "We didn't have a boy, and you think Emily's ugly."
34. (*Black*) "I'm not continuing this conversation through a closed door."

35. (*White*) "Your mother feels the same way,"

Can *Black* avoid: ...**35. "I actually heard your mother say..." 36. "Lying prick." ...36. "At the Christmas party she mentioned the ears, just like your Dad's." 37. "Your family never invites my mother to any gatherings." 37. "You don't want her there." 38. "She's still my mother!" MATE**

35. (*Black*) "What did I say that was so bad?"

The poison as antidote? There is no shame in acting innocent when, in fact, you are innocent.

36. (*White*) She thought that Bill had been mocking Emily's ears to anyone who would listen.
36. (*Black*) "You're the only person he had mentioned this to. I was kidding."

37. (*White*) There was nothing to kid about.

37. (*Black*) Bill lifts Emily from her crib and plants kisses on her ears.

Pointing out that Cynthia's, not his, cousins and aunts were saying the same thing would have been an inappropriate move, merely continuing a bad line toward incompatibility.

38. (*White*) "Do we have to go to your parents' house for dinner Sunday?"

38. (*Black*) This was the first he had heard about it.

39. (*White*) "You should call your parents more."

White matches *Black*'s strength in changing the subject quickly. There is something to be said for conflict avoidance. Again, Larkin - Walsh provides lessons. The strength of Cynthia's father's game was to avoid crushing comments to his wife. How many times had he nearly made questionable moves, sometimes stewing all day over some incident from the previous day, but when the time came to let her have it, say: he would let it pass or simply forget all about. Or sometimes it was blocked out by another of Walsh's grating habits.

39. (*Black*) He doesn't know to which statement to respond to now.

40. (*White*) "I can't believe I forgot to tell you."

Then twist back again to surprise him.

40. (*Black*) "I made plans..."

41. (*White*) She thinks Bill should go ahead with what he had planned to do.
41. (*Black*) "Maybe we should go...."

42. (*White*) Whatever he thinks.
42. (*Black*) They stay home.

DRAW

Bill's voice lacked enough conviction to scare Cynthia into a mistake like **42. "I think we should."** This would have carried the match forward and Bill could then have turned the guilt trip inside out and suggested they take Cynthia's mother to dinner, forcing *White* to a humiliating finish.

Match Score: Pillsbury 0 - 1 - 1   Larkin 1 - 0 - 1

GAME 3 (1987-1999)

Moving Moves

A far-reaching game both in time and space. What seemingly looks bad for Pillsbury, a game of good moves by *Pillsbury*, brings a result that is hard to comment on.

Pillsbury: *White*   Larkin: *Black*

1. (*White*) "How many are coming to this party?"
1. (*Black*) "Judy and her boyfriend, Tom, Frank, Jim. . .do we have enough ice?"

A more traditional start to this game. She knows why he's asking. Will their apartment allow twenty-five to thirty people to mingle comfortably? *Black* counters with reference to a quintessential male trait: never refilling the ice cube trays. *White* will counter with a near meaningless pawn move, to which *Black* could have gainfully replied **2...Who needs a reason to have a party?**

2. (*White*) "What's the occasion?"
2. (*Black*) Cynthia invited over friends and relatives they haven't seen since their wedding day.

3. (*White*) "Tom Gentry works for Century 21 and wants to talk to me about finding a house."

3. (*Black*) "I like this area. There are a bunch of beginning families moving into the neighborhood."

4. (*White*) "We should move out of the apartment and find a bigger place."
4. (*Black*) "Shouldn't we wait for a better mortgage rate?"

5. (*White*) "Mortgage rates might not get any lower" he emphasizes to her.

White lets the economy move for him. The Reagan boom. Half the people on Wall Street were predicting its end. Tom Gentry, the secondary author of the move, half-thought the boom would continue forever. And *Black*'s **"Shouldn't we wait...."** move confirms this commentator's previous observation.

5. (*Black*) "Most of my friends live around here."

6. (*White*) "Wouldn't you like it better near Princeton?"

Students of the match have often remarked on the fact that the sequence of the last two moves was reversed in Game One: see moves **24** and **25**. The moves show how the players' strategies and the relative strength of the moves are contingent upon the focus of a particular game. Pillsbury had tried the **"Wouldn't you like it in Princeton ?"** move at a desperate stage in Game One, but here in the game of "Moves" he uses it as a foundation for a long-term plan to flee urban blight. Likewise, Larkin's "**Most of my friends live around here**" in Game One closed off one potential passage to a draw or victory for *Black*, whereas here we see that she seems, ultimately, to deny the suburbanite's desire for upward mobility.

6. (*Black*) "Good bargains can be gotten in Trenton," Bill had said awhile ago, repeating something he had heard Tom Gentry say to someone else, and which utterance Cynthia now recalled to her husband.

The use of Tom Gentry in moves by both players should be explained. Bill has fortified himself in Cynthia's eyes by having a friend who could help them. However, the impact of *Black*'s third move was undercut by *White's* remembering something said by Bill a long time ago, possibly before Bill got married. Pillsbury had apparently considered but rejected 4. "**Don't try real hard for us, Tom, I don't want to move yet.**" Besides, Larkin could respond to that with: 4...**She checked the telephone book for other realtors, including Remax** or have played the "**Father's friend in real estate**" move because she actually wanted desperately to move. We will see a more sophisticated form of using the other player's moves later in the Match. It should be noted that the game started with Bill being aggressive in the house hunt, then Cynthia taking control to ensure that their move would be to a place she wanted to go.

7. (*White*) With the baby expenses, Bill didn't think they could afford a vacation this year or the next.

7. (*Black*) Cynthia's girlfriend, Sue King, had invited them to her place at the shore next July.

8. (*White*) He might not be able to get off that week.

8. (*Black*) "She said we could come any week."

9. (*White*) "The summer's the heart of our season. I don't see why we have to come to a decision now."

9. (*Black*) She has looked at ten houses in downtown Trenton, none of them cost more than $80,000.

Excellent response when most players would have moved **9...She'd take Emily and go by herself; maybe he'd come down on the weekend.** And so the game continues swimmingly for *Black*. Pillsbury's only response other than deploying his job for duty here was **8. He hated to accept charity**, which was weak considering that he lived with his parents until he got married at age twenty-seven, followed by the acidic **9. He considers Sue King a bad influence on his wife.** Bill suspected Sue of putting the idea of buying a home into Cynthia's head. Besides, with **8. He might not be able to get off that week**, he can rationalize that he was telling the truth. A lesser player than Pillsbury may have played **7. His eldest sister, Judy, offered Bill the use of their vacation house in the Poconos at any time in the winter or summer.** Does it not look as if

Bill could use family resources to provide family getaways and earn the endearing respect of his wife? Today's players, like Pillsbury and Larkin, prefer going it alone, to show their strength, primarily to themselves. Of course, it would have been interesting to see how Bill would have handled Cynthia's likely response: **7...She did not like the mountains and forests and preferred the beach and sun.** Then, again, her move would have incapacitated a beautiful play later in the Match when she took a trip to the Poconos with her girlfriends for a weekend.

10. (*White*) A week later, during Christmas vacation, Bill accompanies Cynthia to look at three houses in Trenton. They liked the third, the end house on a row of ten, and it had a bargain price.
10. (*Black*) They looked at the house again in January and February.

11. (*White*) Joe Tomlin, one of Bill's wedding guests whom they had not seen in a year, works for National City Mortgage and was supervising their mortgage application, waiving the fee.

Compliance with one's opponent's wishes gives the impression that you have planned two or three moves ahead. Pillsbury's father, in Pillsbury - Hutton, used the seemingly strong move **"bought his grandfather's house"** in a similar game, but Hutton neutralized her opponent with a series of five moves to find fault with the wallpaper, rugs, windows, size of the master bedroom, and the lack a basement. However, she never expressed outright disapproval of the purchase because even she was impressed by the initial move. What she managed to do was to sap her spouse's strength defending **"the single most expensive purchase in his life up to that point"** and win the game with relative ease, an amazing feat given that Hutton during the entire game not once made an offensively strong move relative to the final decision to buy any of the four houses and a condominium. Also, Black's next moves continue within the aforesaid cramped position.

11. (*Black*) "We should lock into a rate before it goes up."

12. (*White*) Joe had said that they should wait until a week before closing.
12. (*Black*) A week later, after the rate went from 11 1/2 to 12 percent, she insisted they lock in.

13. (*White*) "Have confidence in Joe. He says the rates will go below 11 percent."

Not: **12. "What do you know about the interest rates?"** or **"You're panicking"** and doubly not: **12. He threatens to back out of buying a house if she keeps butting in.** White does not want to exchange his free run across the marriage board with a petty reaction resulting in blocking his development.

13. (*Black*) She makes sure he knows that she's following Joe's advice. When they locked in at 10¾ % she congratulated herself for not panicking.

14. (*White*) He wants to save several hundred dollars by moving themselves. His friends would help.
14. (*Black*) "You don't want to hurt your back," she said with faint sarcasm.

Black's handling of this idea, to coax him away from moving themselves, deserves praise.

15. (*White*) Bill had read an article in the *Trenton Times* that said large areas of radon were present in Hamilton township, near Princeton, where they had looked at houses.
15. (*Black*) After moving into their Trenton row house, she asks whether the place will be large enough for two children.

16. (*White*) The dog could use a larger backyard.
16. (*Black*) "Did you see that another car parked on the block had a broken window?"

Black might try to isolate her husband's initiative to move

into the city of Trenton, an urban industrial center in decline, by playing the "Fear Gambit." But it is not enough merely to control or occupy Space – you must be able to retain it! The "Fear Gambit" disorients your opponent, yes, but how it affects stability of your next moves can be overlooked.

17. (*White*) He places a triple lock system on the front and back doors of the house; the windows are sealed shut.
17. (*Black*) "Did you hear that? I think someone is downstairs."

18. (*White*) "It's probably the dog."
18. (*Black*) "Bart's beside the bed."

19. (*White*) "If you heard something, he would've started barking."
19. (*Black*) She walks to the baby's room.

20. (*White*) "It must be the house settling."

White rightfully anticipated *Black* not returning with "**Do row houses settle like that?**" Better might have been **20. "Could have been a small earthquake?"** Only then he would have had to worry that *Black* would ask neighbors or read the newspaper to seek some corroboration.

20. (*Black*) Two weeks later, Cynthia's mother's house was broken into.

21. (*White*) "Because she found an earring in the couch?"
21. (*Black*) "She couldn't find one of her Dickens village houses."

22. (*White*) "Someone broke in to steal a fragment of her Christmas display! The old trains she puts around the Christmas tree are probably worth $5000 themselves."
22. (*Black*) Mrs. Larkin insisted that people broke in and made love on her couch. (?)

A chancy pair of moves by *Black* meant to show parallel dangers in the suburbs. A lesser player might not have taken advantage and pursued the point: **21. Bill reminds her of the time Mrs. Larkin called the cops when she thought her handbag had been stolen from the house while she was gardening.** To which *Black* would have returned: **21....Her mother had lived in several foster homes before she was ten years old and always felt insecure.** Then *White* would have made the fatal mistake of a broader attack on his in-laws: **22. "Is that why she's afraid to take any of the larger bridges into Pennsylvania?"** Then *Black*'s knockout punch: **22...."It's tough getting old. Maybe she can't live alone anymore and take care of herself?"** Before long Mrs. Larkin would be unpacking her bags in their guest bedroom, displacing the child soon to inhabit the room. Essentially, *White* is forced into **23. We give her two hundred dollars a month**, and Black: **23...She wouldn't need it if her taxes and utilities weren't so great. 24. I don't see why she has a $400 electric bill every month. 24...Mrs. Larkin keeps the heat on to seventy-seven or -eight degrees.** Before long her moving into her daughter's house will be the result of a Pillsbury's suggestion! And the arrival of another child would mean moving to a larger house, which was really all *Black* would want from winning this game. Yet, could Pillsbury also have wanted the big house? Would a move like **Asks his mother-in-law to move in** be too great a sacrifice? Some argue that what counts is *the reason for the move*, not the move itself: to satisfy his own personal structure of happiness and well-being. Thus, making the same move or "suggestion" during endgame when they're already in the bigger house could in fact clinch victory for Pillsbury, whereas earlier it would bring too much heartache. Why? Because Larkin herself, despite the strong move suggesting that her mother can't take care of herself, would only want her mother around to force his hand. She would in fact argue Pillsbury out of his move and cost herself all chance of winning. **25. Wishes mother-in-law dead** (?) would be unworthy of *White* to even think of, as would **26. Kills Mrs. Larkin but successfully makes her fall down the cellar steps appear like an accident.**

23. (*White*) Why did she believe the 'screwing on the

couch' scenario over any other? Wouldn't thieves have been more interested in her Venetian goblets?

23. (*Black*) *His* family had faults. They would tell you they were coming to visit and then never show up. Or plan some get together and cancel the day before.

24. (*White*) That was them, not him.
24. (*Black*) "I can't get off the phone with your mother in less than forty-five minutes."

25. (*White*) "She likes you."
25. (*Black*) "I like her but she always talks about people I never heard of."

Aggressive but unfocused play by *Black*. She should concentrate on *White*'s inability to perform basic household repairs: planing the back screen door or replacing the washer on the bathroom's leaky faucet. The **"Laziness Gambit"** has proved effective against players who are husbands.

26. (*White*) "She thinks you enjoy the conversation."
26. (*Black*) "You could be just as nice to my mother. When she calls you, you don't even say hello, you just hand me the phone."

27. (*White*) Bill once returned early from work suffering from a stomach virus, but he could not enter his house.

Because Cynthia and Bill worked, her mother would come over every so often to clean the house. This move not only hurt Cynthia's game here in this game but also affected other games when Bill used the **"In-law"** gambit. She was forever defending her mother's actions, the major purpose of this gambit when anyone plays it. In this particular case of apparent altruism by Mrs. Larkin, Bill interpreted it as invasive, not to mention the fact that she cleaned the house so spotlessly that the cleanliness nearly cut into his consciousness. Pillsbury soon appreciated scuff marks on the kitchen floor and dust behind the couch.

27. (*Black*) "Mom thought you were a burglar."

28. (White) Would a burglar ring the front doorbell or bang so loud as to attract the neighbors?
28. (*Black*) Through the walls Cynthia could her neighbor yelling at her children.

29. (*White*) "Don't you think they can hear us?"
29. (*Black*) "Even your mother doesn't feel safe here when she's taking care of Emily. She thought the guy next door was going to come over and beat her up after she had knocked on the wall for them to be quiet."

30. (*White*) Points out that their house is 20 minutes closer to her school than it is to his landscaping business.
30. (*Black*) Receives her third speeding violation in a year.

31. (*White*) He hoped she didn't drive that fast when Emily was in the car.

31. (*Black*) She can get Emily into her school's pre-K program next year at half-cost.

32. (*White*) Buys a book on home improvements.

32. (*Black*) "Didn't Tom say that a property like ours in the city should maintain its value?"

33. (*White*) Bill's boss reported to the staff that he has liver cancer.

33. (*Black*) "You'll get a piece of the business," she responded to the news.

34. (*White*) Bill wants to have another child.

34. (*Black*) She believes with Bill that his future with the landscaping business is now assured.

35. (*White*) "Tom said that because he wanted to sell us this property."

35. (*Black*) Should they think about moving to the suburbs?

Move **34. Bill wants to have another child** has its desired effect on Cynthia. But did the move to Trenton cost them thousands of dollars? Will *Black* or *White* benefit? Does *White* have more surprises for his opponent?

36. (*White*) Tom tells them that they ought to think of selling before the price goes below $60,000.

36. (*Black*) "What's happening with your partnership?"

37. (*White*) At their house warming, he realizes that fewer guests can fit in their house than were able to fit in their apartment. He mentions this a few days later.

37. (*Black*) "I'm pregnant."

Not the move she wanted to make at this point. No strategy behind it. She might have considered sticking with her attack: **37...."Is that bitch Mrs. Chambers going to go against her husband's death wish?"** Which might have forced a retreat by White. 38. **"Nothing's been said."** Countered by: **"Have you asked?"**

38. (*White*) He's visibly happy; his relatives are ecstatic; he desperately wants a boy.

38. (*Black*) She considers having an abortion.

Flailing helplessly, *Black* could have resigned here. Hurting her opponent at his most vulnerable would have led to forceful countermeasures that *Black* would not have had the stamina to handle.

39. (*White*) Bill, Cynthia, Emily, and the newborn, Tara, stay at Bill's mother's for three weeks, between the day they moved from Trenton to the day they moved to Mt.

Laurel, further away from both their workplaces.

39. (*Black*) Mrs. Larkin interprets the move as a means to distance them from her; the feeling became fact when her daughter's family stayed at the Pillsburys' house.

White can only benefit from his mother-in-law's dissatisfaction. More importantly, she voiced her "interpretation" to Bill over the phone. The truth is, though, that the Pillsburys lived closer to Mt. Laurel.

40. (*White*) He travels 20 minutes to work.
40. (*Black*) To get to her school in less than forty-five minutes, she gets more speeding tickets.

41. (*White*) "You kept at me to move out of Trenton. We did. You can't tell me you didn't want this."

Was *White* really saying this? Telling *Black* that it was her idea to move? Yes, she wanted to get away from the working class district but had initially resisted the move because it seemed to come so fast after they had ditched their apartment for the row house. Besides, it seemed obvious that they would lose money on the Trenton house. Actually, it *was* her idea to move to Mount Laurel. Perhaps that was what *White* had meant in move **41**.

43. (*Black*) Cynthia moves into an apartment in New Hope, Pennsylvania, after she separated from Bill, less

than two years after having Tara and moving to Mount Laurel.

44. (*White*) He holds a second housewarming in the Mt. Laurel house when he remarries.

MATE

Black finally realized that her own desires did not really include a house and this husband. When did she know? Certainly before the second child was on the way. Possibly when Bill moved her into the position of thinking she was responsible for their moving into the urban neighborhood, which lost them at least $25,000. And how ominous was it never to get an answer to the question about the partnership in the landscaping business? She didn't even bother to bring it up when it became clear that Mrs. Chambers had sold the landscape franchise to an outsider. So much for Bill's wanting to be independent.

MATCH SCORE: Pillsbury 1 – 1 – 1   Larkin: 1 – 1 – 1

MATCH SUMMARY

Games 4 and 5 lacked the bite, determination, and seriousness of the previous three. Perhaps the couple had compartmentalized their life and memories. These experiences, individually and cumulatively, are treasured fondly, not to mention looked forward to, and provided important markers on the winding path of their marriage. The stage of conflict might also have been intense when they traveled to a favorite summer destination, and it would surprise no one that a dinner in public could erupt into unpleasantness. Yet, going out to dinner and taking the kids to the Jersey shore had less emotional resonance than courtship, child-rearing, and their choice of living quarters.

4. The Vacation Game (1986 - 2000)
The moves of the "Vacation" game figure into other matches. Placed together in a single match, Games 4 and 5 show Bill and Cynthia agreeing too much. In fact, the entire match, and not just in this commentator's opinion, appears to mirror their feelings. White's (Larkin) move **6. Suggests a week at the Atlantis Hotel resort in the Bahamas**, while Black (Pillsbury) responds with the equally economically unaffordable **6. Why not a week at the Hamilton Princess in Bermuda?** They were not married yet. Neither did they have the money. They

merely had a strong faith in the American Express card as if, like college loans, they could stop paying the balance after several years. When the children arrived, the players seemed more purposeful trying to negate the other's dream trip. Pillsbury would suggest **19. He would like to go to Las Vegas and hang around the Sports Bars**, and Larkin would counter 20. **A week at Lake George would be nice**. Pillsbury did not follow up his gambit by selling Sin City as a family resort or suggesting they could visit the Grand Canyon while there, and unaccountably refused to counter the idea of the Lake George trip by informing his wife that Emily was too young to enjoy Fort Ticondaroga. In the endgame, Bill took his new wife to Lake George because, he said to her, that he had always wanted to go there. This indicated that he would try, after a sluggish start in the game, to pull a victory from a position whence both players had no real material advantage. It did not work. His wife wanted to go to San Francisco and that was where they went. He was lucky it didn't cost him the game. Why didn't it? Cynthia went to Australia the year she took a sabbatical (five years after the divorce), did not have sexual relations with any of dozens of willing Aussie men, and was involved in an accident in the outback when her car hit and killed a kangaroo. She suffered a concussion and broken arm. **A Draw.**

MATCH SCORE Pillsbury 1 – 1 – 2   Larkin 1 – 1 – 2

5. The Restaurant Game (1980 - 1994)

The "Restaurant" game devolved into a long and relatively inconsequential Draw marked by stretches of intense action lasting too many moves: Larken (Black) **13.** (a few months before she became pregnant) **"Are we ever going to use the gift certificates my cousin gave us for the Yankee Doodle Taproom?"** As was often the case in this game, tension arose less from the restaurant choice or a restaurant's inadequate menu, stemming more from the manner by which they arrived at a restaurant choice. In this case, unused gift certificates from Christmas time. Pillsbury responded **14. "Are they for $25 or $50?"** He knew their worth ($25) and merely felt obliged to remind Cynthia how cheap her relatives were. Black moved defensively **14. "The place is hardly overpriced."** White: **15. He thought it a little far and out of the way to go.** Black: **15. They could make a day of it and walk around the Princeton campus.** White: **16. "What's there to see?"** Larken played at her husband's intellectual inferiority by suggesting they spend part of the day around the university. White returned to her original move when she re-reasoned why they should go: **16. The Taproom had exactly what Bill liked to eat.** Indeed, Bill's, and to a lesser extent Cynthia's, eating habits limited the breadth of this game. White's first moves had defined the battle: **1. Never eats breakfast. 2. During his college years, he lived on french fries, cola, burgers, and grilled sticky buns. 3. Never wore a jacket to a restaurant until the Rehearsal** dinner. Black's appetites were low key: **1. Started each day with a bowl of Quaker Oats. 2. During college, she was a vegetarian for two years. 3. She never ate Chinese and Indian food until she dated Bill.** Thus, the International House of Pancakes never became a venue in this match. Although Bill liked to think so, hoping, one would suppose, that it would give him an early advantage in the game, he was not responsible for Cynthia giving up her Vegetarian folly. Likewise, Cynthia never could realize an advantage by having, as she thought she would, Bill change his egregious eating habits.They rarely took Emily to a restaurant, agreeing among themselves not to inflict a scourge, an ill-comported child, that they themselves could not tolerate while eating in public, but they still managed to get a few evenings out. Hence, much of the middle part of the "Restaurant" game actually dealt with the availability of, and anxiety over, babysitters. Once their second child appeared, Bill and Cynthia ceased going to restaurants and brought the game to a crashing halt and DRAW.

MATCH SCORE Pillsbury 1 – 1 – 3   Larkin 1 – 1 – 3

GAME 6 (1983-1990)

His and Her Freedom Game

A difficult game for anyone to win...or lose. Every move could have a question mark or an exclamation point beside it. Nerves of steel or absolutely no nerve direct these players to the point of recognizing there is another player.

    Larkin *White*   Pillsbury *Black*

1. (*White*) "You don't mind if I date other guys."
1. (*Black*) "I don't want to go out with any other woman but Cynthia," he tells his best friend, Fran Clifton.

Had these moves *actually been addressed* to the other player, the outcome could have been different. Larkin's is an accepted opening. She assumed, and her opponent might live up to her assumption, her boyfriends would not remain loyal and, thus, her development would have been hampered by an opening like **1. "You're the only man for me."** Pillsbury's move seems incongruous to his early reputation to screw anything with a hole between its legs, but, like Larkin's, is fairly standard to many relationships that evolve into a Marriage Match.

2. (*White*) She first makes love to Bill after a party where they had been drinking grain alcohol and smoking reefer.

2. (*Black*) He calls her for a date the next afternoon.

3. (*White*) She does not go to bed with him again until six months after their first date.

3. (*Black*) He leaves her apartment not more than an hour after the first ten times they have sex.

4. (*White*) Introduces Bill to her family for their first Christmas together.

4. (*Black*) "I rarely meet Bill's girlfriends," said Mrs. Pillsbury, a year and a half after they had been going out.

Who proved more serious in the relationship first? *White's* move has a professional air about it, as if Larkin understood her long term goals. However, *Black's* response coupled with his opening move has an underlying power which few can appreciate. *Black's* sister, in Levine - Pillsbury, had a situation where neither player knew whether the parental introduction move would have cramped their movements during their "His and Her Pleasure" Game. Levine is Jewish and knew all the family shit he would have to face for marrying a gentile. He unwisely postponed all family meetings until the wedding day, with sad results. The ceremony took place in a Catholic Church and the Levine grumbling started before the couple came up the aisle. Wisely, Judy Pillsbury had introduced Josiah to her parents six months before and had him face moves like **"Are the children going to be brought up Christian?"** and

"**Do you have any trouble with Christmas?**" and, from a Pillsbury aunt, "**Have the Jews ever apologized for killing Jesus?**" His answer: "**I believe the Jews are waiting for an apology from Christianity for being labeled Christ-killers,**" while satisfying to read about, pretty much left him on the defensive because the aunt apparently had the largest fortune and, subsequent to his move, no longer considered Judy her favorite niece.

5. (*White*) She liked to smoke a joint before sex to enhance her orgasm.
5. (*Black*) Bill felt it important to intensify the woman's pleasure during sexual experiences for the first few years.

6. (*White*) "When are you going to get a steady job?" she asks when they are out of college for a year. "You can't be so cavalier about everything."
6. (*Black*) He was willing to take a steady job if it meant she would consider marrying him.

A prelude to his infamous early move in Game One: **2. "I always figured we would."**

7. (*White*) She does not want to have children immediately.
7. (*Black*) He thought having children was the reason a couple got married.

How they moved and what they really wanted are two

separate issues. For example, in Game 1, when Pillsbury responded to **13... "I made an appointment to see Dr. Pearlman."** with **14. "Do you think you are pregnant?"** (?) belies his actual joy and her actual disappointment over the pregnancy. We can see how his response in this game has been conditioned by Larkin's repertoire. Master players must know when to modify their attitudes to meet a crisis.

8. (*White*) "Why do we always see the movies you want to see?"
8. (*Black*) He thought she said she wanted to see *Police Academy.*

9. (*White*) "It was your type of movie."
9. (*Black*) "Why don't you go to the movies you like by yourself?"

Black's tack is logical, sound, and getting him absolutely nowhere. *White* knows she has a good thing going and continues despite getting little or no long term material or position superiority. Clifton - Chalmers Match avoided this problem for Clifton because Fran was disinterested in movies and the non-sports versions of entertainment. The struggle between the two took part largely on gridiron issues. Gentry - Smith, on the other hand, completely agreed on the types of movies they would see: nothing from the art houses, nothing with the tinge of "independent filmmaking." Pillsbury - Hutton and Larkin - Walsh, of course, as was the wont of many of the older generation's Matches, deference to the woman's choice of movies before marriage transposed into the exact opposite inside the marriage.

10. (*White*) "Would you go to the movies without me?"
10. (*Black*) "Maybe to ones I know you wouldn't like."

11. (*White*) "But I go to the ones I think you like!"
11. (*Black*) "I watch your television shows."

12. (*White*) "Shows you enjoy."
12. (*Black*) Not always. Many of them were excruciatingly bad.

Better: **12... There hasn't been an all-female movie remotely equal to the numerous wonderful all-male movies like** *The Great Escape*, *The Dirty Dozen*, *Von Ryan's Express*, *Kelly's Heroes*, *Dirty Harry*, *Reservoir Dogs*, *The Bridge on the River Kwai*, *The French Connection*, *The Wild Bunch*. It is laughable to think that one would counter with: **13.** *The Hours*, *Steel Magnolias*, *Fried Green Tomatoes*, *Mona Lisa Smile*. No, the only plausible response is the so-called chick flick, which needs men in it to initiate romance. Yes, romance, the best defense against all-male movie bravado.

13. (*White*) Her philosophical musing: Isn't marriage

supposed to be about mutual sacrifice? Enjoying sacrifice? Fifty-fifty?

13. (*Black*) Bill did not see, feel, or experience how he was always getting his way when she said that he was.

14. (*White*) We're never doing anything I like. We spend more time with your friends.

A subtle change of strategy. *White* goes from the particular, movies, to the general, anything. *Black* cannot move except defensively and only hopes that his defense can put pressure on her.

14. (*Black*) It occurred to him: if they are going to quibble about every thing they do, worrying about everything being for one or the other's benefit, maybe they shouldn't be getting married. Instead, he infers she might be a little selfish.

We *would have* applauded him for having the courage to say what had to be said at the risk of losing the game, at the greater risk of ending the Match, which is to say *breaking the engagement*, before it had a chance to reach a championship level. In any case, we also congratulate Pillsbury for not having uttered his naked thoughts. Indeed, should the Match have gone on longer than it had, there promised to be a game of the things they wanted to say to the other but wisely held their tongues.

15. (*White*) Cynthia cries, believing she is not a selfish person.

Does this move ever fail? It might not always succeed but Pillsbury must remain on the defensive until, frankly, he can counter at some point in the Match with **I don't give a fuck what she thinks**, but not at the point when he really doesn't give a fuck what she thinks.

15. (*Black*) She used to like it when he did *that*.

What "*that*" is could be a number of things, many of which she never really liked. This move anticipates *White*'s next perfectly, something Larkin kept handy when Pillsbury might be getting a case of self-confidence.

16. (*White*) Buys the book *Women Who Love Too Much*.
16. (*Black*) "I thought I was more like Peter Pan."

Sarcasm works best, as we witness here, when the opponent does not recognize it as such. This was a rare play for Pillsbury. He will eventually prefer the tactic: repeat what your spouse said previously, that is, throw back onto your opponent her very words. Larkin proved no slouch with this either.

17. (*White*) "Do you take anything seriously besides your stupid Fantasy Football League?"

17. (*Black*) "The problem is that you don't have any hobbies."

18. (*White*) A Bahamian vacation on a private island. One week. Nude sunbathing. Her idea.
18. (*Black*) "Do you like being married?" he asks while they sunbathe on a pink sand beach.

19. (*White*) "It's sort of a letdown. I mean, I'm not unhappy. I thought our lives would change drastically."

Better or not, experts would have liked to have seen **19. She never thought she could get used to shit stains in his underwear.** In other words, she expected him to be different. Thus, should he directly respond to the **"shit stain"** move, White could start a heavy salvo with **20. You make the fucking bed --** either spoken or thought.

19. (*Black*) "It'll be different when we have kids."

20. (*White*) "That's when it will really be a drag. No Bahamas."
20. (*Black*) "Most of our friends are married. We'll fit in better when we have a family."

21. (*White*) She did not believe people could be perpetually happy. Something has to go wrong.

Is *White* whistling in the wind? Or does she know where the Match will go and ultimately how it would be decided? Just thinking this move is dangerous, however. She could start interpreting his moves wrongly and subsequently adversely affect the quality of her own. Also, such an idle move could allow *Black* to take the offensive, which he does.

21. (*Black*) "You mean I get on your nerves."

22. (*White*) "I don't get on your nerves, do I?"
22. (*Black*) "What do you want from marriage if you don't want children?"

23. (*White*) She did not want kids right away. She wanted her freedom a few more years. She wanted a flat stomach without stretch marks until she was thirty-three.
23. (*Black*) He did not mind his freedom limited by the responsibilities of family life. Living for the kids should be the husband's and wife's primary goal.

You might think these last few moves would been made earlier in their relationship when the couple "thought" their moves were an attempt to get know each other better. Other games by the Masters, especially those to whom destiny was kinder, had similar moves as earlier as the third and fourth during this Freedom game. One recalls the great match between Rosen and Huessy, when Rosen knew from the beginning **3. Attaches his wife's name to his own when they are married.** One might think that the very structure of these matches means only strife. This may be true in the modern game; however, before the twentieth century, married solidarity could incorporate love and strife more easily. Some will say, and as hard as it is to believe this as it might seem, there is some truth to it, that many of the early Masters did not care about winning. Some of the old timers have commented in memoirs that the biggest difference between Matches then and now is that now players want to know where they stand with the other nearly all the time. "This is tragedy of the modern game," writes one, "the games cannot avoid desperate attempts to defeat one's opponent."

24. (*White*) When it happens, she tells her friends getting pregnant is the best thing to happen to her.
24. (*Black*) "I thought we were going to wait a few years."

25. (*White*) Tells her fellow teachers not to tell the students she is pregnant but then tells them herself even before her belly noticeably swells.
25. (*Black*) His friends kid him that he won't be coming out with them as often. He denies it but eventually finds that he has less desire to see many of them anymore.

A move perhaps more involuntary or not, but ultimately effective in convincing *White* that he lives for her pleasure.

26. (*White*) Suffers morning sickness.

26. (*Black*) Gives up smoking cigarettes but will occasionally sneak out to the backyard and have one.

27. (*White*) She smells the cigarette odor on his clothes and complains that he is indulging in a pleasure forbidden to her.

27. (*Black*) "I'm not doing it in front of you."

Does *Black* really believe what he just said? Does he realize how grossly he is flaunting his pleasure at her? Does not the sacrifice of her pleasure, via the pregnancy, account for any inclination for reciprocal sacrifice?

28. (*White*) "I'd like to get away from Emily for a few hours."

28. (*Black*) "Maybe you shouldn't go back to school so soon."

Right move, wrong game....

29. (*White*) "We can't afford it."

29. (*Black*) "We'll give up a few things."

30. (*White*) She reminds him of his attitude from the day they had bought the changing table.

Each player faces a dilemma. To gain a piece, to get what

one wants, *Black* must sacrifice more than he could imagine. White's pursuit of a career and putting off having a baby has camouflaged her worrying about paying bills. If a move seems too forceful, like Bill's claiming **1. "I don't want to go out with anyone other than Cynthia"**, or Cynthia's **22. "I don't get on your nerves, do I?"**, we could do worse than question the players' sincerity. A strong, insincere move in the endgame can be very effective, but generally a player cannot build a defense or offense on or around an insincere move. When the players are most sincere, the words have difficulty being verbalized and rolled into play. *Black*'s next sentiment would be the perfect rejoinder to *White*'s blast from a past game. Unfortunately, he could not spit it out.

30. (*Black*) He could abide the changing table purchase if there had been an opportunity to use it again.

31. (*White*) Her mother volunteers to look after Emily and saves the couple the cost of Day Care.
31. (*Black*) "*My* mother said she would help."

32. (*White*) Cynthia wants Bill to share in the making of meals, especially dinner.

Black must defend against *White*'s follow up: **33. Cuts out recipes from the newspaper or 33. Becomes addicted to cooking shows Saturdays on PBS and expects Bill to be**

at her side, and **34. Wants Bill to go food shopping with her**, the latter leading to deep unpleasantness for everyone and further eroding the marriage foundation in an effort to get her way or, basically the same, resisting her getting her way.

32. (*Black*) "I'm going to make a tuna salad sandwich."

33. (*White*) "Don't put mayonnaise in it."
33. (*Black*) "I only put a little on."

34. (*White*) She wants to mix the tuna into her lettuce greens.
34. (*Black*) He will give her the tuna first and then mix in the mayonnaise.

35. (*White*) She waves him away. It is not worth the bother splitting what's in the can, it is too small.
35. (*Black*) "It won't be hard to make two separate batches."

36. (*White*) Forget it, I'm not hungry.
36. (*Black*) He suggests ordering Chinese.

37. (*White*) "We can't have Chinese every other day. I've nearly lost my taste for it."
37. (*Black*) "Get extra spicy."

38. (*White*) They spend too much money on take out and

going to restaurants.

38. (*Black*) "You're not the greatest cook."

Note the avoidance of sarcasm, especially the undetectable kind. Better: **38... "Honey, you aren't so bad a cook."** The Mayonaisse issue will return at a a much more sensitive time.

39. (*White*) "Emily wants to go to Disney World."
39. (Black) "She's only two. How does she know where she wants to go?"

Probably better, for inflicting more damage, is **39..."You want to go there?"** and thus preventing 40. **As if you wouldn't want to shoot over to Universal Studios.** But what he said works just as well. *White* then returns to the former conversation as quickly as she swerved from it.

40. (*White*) "Are you telling me you don't like anything I cook?"
40. (*Black*) "You're worried about take out Chinese and then want to blow our savings on a fat-ass vacation."

Smartly, Black does not take the bait by coming back with **40...Not that your mother could have taught you anything about it.**

41. (*White*) Does he have any alternatives?

41. (*Black*) "We could get a house at the shore for a week."

42. (*White*) Cynthia was sick of the seashore before she had graduated from high school.   (?)

Weak response. First, *Black* didn't believe her. Second, *White* didn't believe it herself, as moves in other games would bear out. Better: **42. "Won't it cost too much?"** and if *Black* counters with a sturdy: **42...No fucking way"**, White responds: **43. Shouldn't we think about saving for our children's education?** Even better: Larkin could work her in-laws to say the exact thing to Bill. It would not turn a (?) into a (!) but certainly would have Black on the defensive.

42. (*Black*) It seemed more manageable than taking a kid on a plane, he thought

43. (*White*) "Maybe our folks can take care of Emily."
43. (*Black*) "Won't you miss her?"

44. (*White*) She thought it imperative that they should be alone together to reinvigorate the romance in their marriage.   (?)

What was she thinking? The couple made love regularly, a couple times a week, average, until a year before Tara, that is, around the time she made this move to reinvigorate the romance. First, she believed the lovemaking would smooth over what she thought were their differences. What she overlooked, though, was the fact that the differences were nothing less than a growing contempt for each other. He had seen her cool toward him, in the lovemaking and avoidance of lovemaking, but thought it a natural process of the marriage, which allows him to make the next move.

44. (*Black*) "You don't think I'm attracted to you anymore?"
44. (White) RESIGNS

He believes that he himself is the problem and the eventual solution would be to raise the bar of "her pleasure." White is defenseless. She has lost control and knows subsequent moves will lead to her **"I'm pregnant," she tells him at breakfast**, and **Cynthia wants to get an abortion**. She is trapped into the "her pleasure" game, whereas *Black*'s "his pleasure" game falls aside when it becomes decidedly not about what is best for "his pleasure."

MATCH SCORE: Pillsbury 2 – 1 – 3   Larkin: 1 – 2 – 3

MATCH SUMMARY II

Games 7 & 8

Game 7

The Schooling Game (1992- 1997)

Inevitably, Pillsbury started the "Schooling" game with **1. "Pre-K is the most ridiculous thing I ever head of"** and **2. Bill's parents thought their son had developed very well in Kindergarten.** These traditional moves follow the logic: what worked well in my childhood will certainly follow with my own children. Larkin's professional experience made her skeptical of "the way things used to be," especially in all matters pertaining to education. Her initial defense of her position, however, took a different tack (after humoring Bill with early moves appealing to reason): **3. "Have you compared the costs of daycare to early schooling?"** He had not but he resumed the battle when it came to the choice of elementary school: **5. Emily should go to a Catholic school. !** Larkin had not expected this, given his easy capitulation to her earlier economic argument. The next moves included involving in-laws beyond their respective parents, "involving" meaning mostly indirect use of their extended families' experiences in public and Catholic schools. Bill was partly unnerved by Cynthia's resistance to his demand since she was a product of the parochial school system. What he hadn't immediately realized was that going to a Catholic school with mostly nuns as your teachers may often serve to make funny reminisces but the experience itself had left a deeper feeling of animosity and disgust. Bill still worked hard developing his position, especially with the apparently undeniable claims: **11. "There's better discipline in Catholic schools"** and, what he thought was the kicker, **12. "Even you said that any of your students coming from public schools had terrible grammar."** ! The biggest threat to Bill's movements came five years later when Emily transferred to the private school where Cynthia taught in move **15.** However, she could only get one-fourth of the tuition taken out. Bill responded: **16. At least we saved a little money.** Her miscalculation was based on trusting what the school administration had told her a few years before. When it came to high school, again Cynthia was frustrated. Emily wanted to go to the Catholic high school because most of her friends went there and didn't care that her education would be free at Cynthia's school. Cynthia navigated the middle game not realizing that her daughter might not want to be near her mother at school (did this mean that her wanting to be with her friends was a lie?). As for the endgame, concerning the education of their second child, Tara, both players took the line of least resistance, perhaps because they were separated. Tara would attend public school to save the household budget. A costly, ass backward victory, indeed, for Cynthia.

MATCH SCORE: Pillsbury 2 – 2 – 3   Larkin: 2 – 2 – 3

Game 8

You are what you eat and drink Game (1984 - 2005)

Related to the earlier "Restaurant" game, the "You Are What You Eat and Drink" Game is less serious and, at the same time, destined to have a winner. Not that either player ever gave much thought to it. Who thinks how one will look after thirty or thirty-five years? The endgame makes for curious, at times furious, attempts to look better, lose weight, and combat various diseases, like diabetes. In other words, looking much older than you are or being heavier (much heavier) than your (ex-) spouse determines everything. The only chance to avoid defeat would have been staying together for life. Cynthia's early moves could not gain traction, partly due to her indifference to the imperative of "prettying herself" and, to use her mother's phrase, "dolling herself up." Pillsbury countered nimbly: **...1. Bill's mother wouldn't let him eat between meals and he rarely had candy, which he carried deep into his adult life, ...2. He was always skinny, even in college, ...3. Relatives remarked about him until the age of thirty-five that Bill could eat anything in great amounts and never gain weight.** Following the start of the feminist movement, Cynthia's generation of women (the ones she hung around with) eschewed the bra except when she taught, suckled babies in public, wore significantly less makeup, made the girdle and other restrictive undergarments obsolete. Yes, such moves were mollified by Bill's acceptance of her life choices, though he did not significantly subscribe to feminist ideas and the struggle for equality with men. One's eating habits are easily influenced by the proximity of one's spouse's fasting, gluttony, or whatever manner of indulging themselves took. Cynthia drank beer and ate potato chips and pretzels seemingly to keep up with Bill, despite her worries about loss of brain cells and high blood pressure. He would starve with her. and let her know he was starving, when she decided to try NutriSystems weight loss program and, of course, Weight Watchers. The latter he sorely resented because it started after their second child and when his grip on the marriage was slipping. Thank God, he felt, that his wife wasn't a recovering alcoholic, denying him the fun of getting tipsy. Though her abstaining from alcohol could have been the one way of defeating him, that is, making him suffer, relatively speaking, for her better health. Those brief spurts of being on the wagon during her two pregnancies positioned her nicely against Bill, but when the time came, she threw herself more enthusiastically into the hard liquor, especially, and added significant pounds to her figure, pounds she could never lose. If Bill hadn't been interested in her looks, she may have gained a draw.

MATCH SCORE: **Pillsbury 3 – 2 – 2   Larkin 2 – 3 – 3**

Game 9 (1981-1995)

His and Her Friends Game

You can choose your friends but can you choose or even control their moves?

    Pillsbury *White*   Larkin *Black*

1. (*White*) "You won't be able to shake her now that you have slept with her," says Fran Clifton, Bill's best friend in college.

1. (*Black*) "Now that he's slept with you, you will never see him again," Cynthia's best friend, Clara Browne, tells her.

2. (*White*) "She came on to me," Todd Feldman told Fran, before Fran spoke to Bill about Cynthia.

2. (*Black*) "He's not very intellectual," Sara Gibbons says to Clara, "he definitely won't be able to keep up with Cynthia."

3. (*White*) Bill wants to stay with Cynthia and not go to the Poconos with his friends for the weekend.

3. (*Black*) Cynthia and several girlfriends go to the Poconos a month later.

4. (*White*) Clara tells Fran that Cynthia was hung up on some Greek guy.

A sign of weakness, on the surface, when a friend consorts with and reveals personal information to one's opponent's friend. That Clara and Fran are married only partly mitigates the betrayal.

4. (*Black*) "I think Demetrius works in a hotel in the Poconos as a waiter," Sara tells Clara.

5. (*White*) Fran marries Clara when he is twenty-three and has three children before thirty. (!)

Bill's friend puts pressure on Cynthia to reproduce similarly.

5. (*Black*) "Remember when Trisha ran way with the Egyptian guy. She met him in Dijon during her semester in France," Clara tells Sara.

The suggestion from Cynthia's side of the board appears to be this: she should have taken a chance with Demetrius. At the least, she might have delayed her marriage to Bill or not even married him. The latter possibility exposes the inherent weakness of having friends at all. Black's subsequent move (**6.** . .) reinforces this.

6. (*White*) All other fantasy league members are married and have children.
6. (*Black*) Teresa Mills, Cynthia's best friend in grade

school, slashed the tires of a former boyfriend's car outside a bar.

7. (*White*) Fran tells his wife that Cynthia busts Bill's balls about his job all the time.
7. (*Black*) "She always does what Bill wants to do," Clara responds.

8. (*White*) "He nearly owns the business. What more does she want?"
8. (*Black*) "He's never getting that business," Clara told Sara. "I know Mrs Chambers, her husband owns the business."

9. (*White*) "He got screwed out of it. He was promised it a couple years ago."
9. (*Black*) "Cynthia's probably happy they didn't have to take out a loan to buy the franchise."

10. (*White*) "We all go to Bill's house to watch the football game," says Mark Gibbons to his wife, Sara, "and Cynthia decides to stick around and be miserable."
10. (*Black*) "Greg Mueller broke their glass table. She has a right to be miserable."

11. (*White*) "It was an ash tray." (!)

Move **10**. . . is outmaneuvered not by giving a truthful account of the accident but by reducing the offense making Cynthia so miserable.

11. (*Black*) Suzanne Gallagher, a colleague of Cynthia's, her husband, and three other couples go to a Spanish restaurant in Trenton, after which Suzanne's husband, Jeff, pays the bill.

12. (*White*) Bill and the other husbands all tried to grab the check but perhaps did not try hard enough.
12. (*Black*) Suzanne's husband works for Johnson & Johnson.

13. (*White*) "That asshole named his dog, Doug," Fran tells Todd, who was not at the restaurant, and who didn't know what "Doug" referred to.
13. (*Black*) Jeff has finished writing a novel and would like Cynthia to take a look at it.

14. (*White*) "Bill was quiet the other night at the restaurant," Suzanne says to Cynthia.

It seems Jeff meddles with many marriage games and matches during and after dinner. Perhaps that's his mission in life, pursued despite the deleterious effects on his own Match, one short-lived such as not to matter in the grand scheme of things!

14. (*Black*) Paul, a gay friend of Cynthia's, asks her to go to dinner with him.

15. (*White*) "My wife saw Cynthia with another guy last week," Fran tells Todd.
15. (*Black*) Todd's wife mentions the dinner date to Cynthia and they have a good laugh.

16. (*White*) Mark Gibbons calls Cynthia a phony to several of his and Bill's mutual friends
16. (*Black*) Sara tells Clara that Paul told her that Cynthia is tired of living with Bill.

17. (*White*) "She puts on her airs of being a literary scholar when she's only a high school English teacher."
17. (*Black*) "You don't like her because she criticized Reagan at the picnic last week. Besides, she can't talk to Bill about anything."

Black is showing life after taking many severe blows from Pillsbury's confidantes.

18. (*White*) Bill's friends think it's the worst thing to happen to Bill that Cynthia gets pregnant.
18. (*Black*) Cynthia's friends console themselves with the thought that Bill and Cynthia will finally have something in common with Emily to take care of.

19. (*White*) "We haven't seen the Pillsburys in years," Mark says to Sara.

19. (*Black*) "Cynthia stopped calling me after her first kid," Paul tells Suzanne.

We are now seeing how the first two games of Pillsbury – Larkin are having an effect on the Match barely suspected when those games were in play.

20. (*White*) "Her mother is killing the marriage," says Todd to his wife.

20. (*Black*) "I wonder if they will get rid of Bart," Jeff says to Suzanne.

21. (*White*) "Even Bill doesn't like her politics," says Mark.

21. (*Black*) "Paul is the only man she can talk to," Sara says to Clara.

22. (*White*) "If she would only talk about something Bill was interested in," Mark adds.

22. (*Black*) Suzanne and Cynthia are not talking since Suzanne transferred to a public school.

23. (*White*) "She's getting double the pay, now. Cynthia didn't appreciate that kind of career move before she tried it herself," Todd pontificates one evening before they leave to have dinner at the Pillsburys.

23. (*Black*) "Cynthia won't even talk about Suzanne. I think Bill and Suzanne had a thing."

24. (*White*) "You're imagining it. Suzanne's happily married."
24. (*Black*) "She divorced Jeff six months ago."

25. (*White*) "Jeff dumped Suzanne for his secretary," Mark tells Sara.
25. (*Black*) Sara heard that Suzanne stopped by the house after the separation and found Jeff in the backyard with his secretary and both were naked.

26. (*White*) "I wonder if her name was Candace," Fran tells Todd, who is as clueless about this remark as he was about the dog being called Doug.
26. (*Black*) "She's better off without him," Clara tells Fran. "He gave her the papers and Suzanne did not have a hint that anything was wrong."

27. (*White*) Fran told Mark that Suzanne was on the rebound and noticed that Bill wasn't too happy.
27. (*Black*) Joan Talbert, a teacher at Cynthia's school, mentioned to her husband that Suzanne was always asking about Bill after the party at the restaurant. That made Cynthia suspicious.

Finally, the jealousy move, meaning "the apparent jealousy" move. We're all among friends. Yes, but who knows what's going on in their minds. In Jeff's Match, he acted outside the friendship, but never inside the work sphere. And how many spheres do these couples have to worry about? It's a good thing that most moves in these Matches aren't deliberate or been planned ahead. Really, they can barely see one move ahead and generally forget previous moves.

28. (*White*) Mark cannot believe anything happened between Bill and Suzanne. How much of a "play" could it have been?
28. (*Black*) Suzanne asked Bill to lunch behind Cynthia's back. "At least," Clara tells Fran, "Bill knew about Cynthia's dinner with Paul."

29. (*White*) Todd defends Bill. Didn't his friend accept the invitation? Didn't he tell Cynthia about it, eventually?
29. (*Black*) "I understand that he was encouraging Suzanne," Clara says to Sara. "I think that's the reason Bill and Cynthia split."

It was not.

30. (*White*) "There was more going on," Mark tells Sara. "Don't blame it all on that."

30. (*Black*) "She is more sore at him," says Todd's wife. "She can't even bring herself to talk about it."

31. (*White*) "If she felt so badly about it," Fran tells Todd, "how did she get pregnant the second time?"
31. (*Black*) "This happened after she got pregnant with Tara," Todd is informed by his wife.

32. (*White*) "That's why I think Cynthia's a phony," Mark tells Todd. "She doesn't want to have kids when they should and has one exactly when she shouldn't."
32. (*Black*) "Bill kept on and on about Emily wanting a sister," Sara told Suzanne, when they bumped into each other at Macy's.

33. (*White*) Bill told Todd that Cynthia had become distant since the second child, meaning that they hadn't had sex.
33. (*Black*) Clara claims Bill never got over his first love.

34. (*White*) "At least Bill is going to a counselor with Cynthia," says Mark.
34. (Black) Sara and Clara say it's bullshit; Bill is supposedly very belligerent at the meetings .

35. (*White*) "Bill's not that type," Mark counters. "Cynthia's making him out to be a monster so she can take the kids."
35. (*Black*) Bill's drug use becomes an issue among Cynthia's girlfriends.

The irresponsibility of the move can't be blamed on Cynthia. You'd think they would want her to win the Match with Bill.

36. (*White*) "Bill's building a new family by getting married again. He never wanted to leave Cynthia," says Fran.
36. (*Black*) Now you are making her the monster," his wife tells him. "Can't a woman want a career, let alone a decent conversation? She can't always be talking football."

37. (*White*) The couple hardly sees Bill since his marriage to the Virgin.
37. (*Black*) Cynthia hasn't deserted her friends.

Again, a move that is not as strong as it appears.

38. (*White*) "She let him have the majority custody," Mark tells Fran. "She should have thought of that first."
38. (*Black*) Her friends used to like Bill; never saw the creepy side of him, that is, until he didn't let Cynthia have the kids one weekend.

39. (*White*) Cynthia ignored some of Bill's friends at the mall.
39. (*Black*) The women tried to denigrate Bill, speaking about his still being in the landscaping business.

40. (*White*) Bill's friends defend him, might even still like him, though they haven't seen him for many years.
40. (*Black*) RESIGNS

Once one understands what matters in friendship, especially not seeing your friends often or not at all, then Larkin's loss here makes a little sense.

MATCH SCORE Pillsbury 4 – 2 – 3   Larkin 2 – 4 – 3

MATCH SUMMARY III

Game 10

The Parents Game (1987 - 2005)

Many matches have their bloodiest conflicts – literally, not figuratively – when the parents weigh in on their children's marital situations. Fighting may range from approving or disapproving the choice of spouse, the children – Bill's and Cynthia's parents showed admirable restraint here – to the inevitable money problems faced by most middle class couples. If the parents don't die in due time, how the couple should deal with parents suffering from Alzheimers and dementia enters the endgame. Pillsbury and Larkin's parents prepared for their own parents' old age their kids could not fathom. Cynthia's mother lived into her 90s, dying long after her daughter's marriage ended, never needing Assisted Living care or a nursing home, despite her fragile psyche. Move **25. Cynthia discovers her mother's bank accounts, yes, more than one, had accumulated over \$300,000.** This would be money Bill would never see; worse, the money would have been available at the time he was trying to start his own landscaping business. Cynthia's move, despite its strength, still left her discombobulated because she couldn't understand where the money had come. Mr

Larkin's death only provided a small portion of this sum from a life insurance policy back in the 1970s. Not to mention, Mrs Larkin always complained about having to pay property tax and utility bills. In a move that came some time after the Match was over, Cynthia received half her mother's estate, which was bolstered when Mrs Larkin sold her house several years before she died. As for the move: while her mother lived into her nineties, Cynthia, more than her siblings, attended to many of her mother's needs, including upkeeping the house: new kitchen floor, new roof, and a complete overhaul of the electrical outlets and wires. An underlying issue in Parent games is overbearing siblings and the inevitability that one of them seems dedicated to making the parents miserable. In Bill's case, it was a sister, Patricia, whom no one spoke about, her absence in previous and subsequent games suggests this, because she was a drug addict for thirty years, eventually matriculating to heroin. Bill's parents' guilt over Patricia, blaming themselves for her weak upbringing, led to their aiding Patricia financially at every bad turn, despite their daughter's visible contempt for them because of weak upbringing or, in other words, her playing on their source of guilt. For twenty years this went on, effectively destroying the emotional fabric of the marriage, ending mercifully only when Patricia fell two flights down the outdoor fire escape, most likely higher on drugs than she had ever been. End result: move **28... Bill's father depleted several IRA accounts** to support his daughter before her death. One might wonder how either one of our competitors could alone have survived this game. It's amazing that Cynthia could play on after **15 Mrs Larkin would soon place a dead pet in the oven, with a cat and several parakeets to follow over the years, and turn up the temperature to 200 to 225 degrees Fahrenheit, believing the warmth would revive them.** How could Bill lose? Mrs Larkin's paranoia animated many family gatherings and created extreme embarrassment for Cynthia, especially after **6. Mrs Larkin calls Mr Pillsbury an asshole after a brief discussion about the relative availability of money after World War II.** She had preceded the move with **5. "My family didn't see much money then," said Mrs Larkin. 5...** "Your husband would've agreed with me," said Mr Pillsbury. He invoked a dead husband (!!) to win his point. That's one of the follies of marriage competition. Trying to win in the moment at the expanse of losing the entire game or Match. Mrs Larkin's thoughts, words, and actions became the center around which Bill and Cynthia's marriage revolved. Bill complained bitterly because Cynthia's mother seemed to be at the house so often. However, he was heard saying **45...**"She really wasn't such a bad person. She just had issues." Didn't he realize that his post-Match Bi-polar issues might have been traced to her presence in his life? Or was he unable to understand the truth because time eroded the original formidable cornerstones of his memory? Also unhelpful to Bill's endgame were the problems he would have with "the Virgin's" parents: **52...Bill's new father-in-law had served prison time for embezzling from a charity.** White collar crime, yes, served at a "country club" prison, but still a humiliation hard to shake, not so much for him as for Bill! **53...He often felt his friends, his neighbors, cousins, and especially Cynthia thought of him as being on the same plane.** His Resigning the game was only a few moves away.

MATCH SCORE Pillsbury 4 – 3 – 3   Larkin 3 – 4 – 3

NOTE:
Halfway point. Pillsbury missed a great opportunity to get within one win and taking the Match. Who would have guessed his new in-laws would have such significance given their brief appearance not only in the Game but their only game in the entire Match? The Marriage matches are typically fraught with the unexpected, with the weak being victorious, and great moves having deleterious effects. Larkin will waste little time squaring things up.

Quick Resignation Game

This brief game shocked all observers. However, once you play out the possibilities, there is no hope for *White*. Indeed, no one since has been able find the moves to avoid the path to defeat.

Pillsbury *White*   Larkin   *Black*

1. (*White*) John Evian Pillsbury came to America in the late 1740s. His grandson became a follower of Charles Gradison Finney and established the Pillsbury branch of the family with an evangelical streak.

1. (*Black*) The Supremacy Act, 1534, establishes the Anglican Church, which did not strongly deviate from the rituals of the Catholic Church.

2. (*White*) Bill's parents baptize him and his sisters. The family reads the Bible every evening.

2. (Black) Mr. Larkin converts to Catholicism with apparent ease and marries Joan Walsh.

3. (*White*) "Mom, why don't we celebrate my birthday?"

3. (*Black*) Cynthia crowns the statue of the Blessed Mother during her fourth grade May Procession.

4. (*White*) "Bill, never marry a non-Christian, but even more, do NOT marry a Catholic," Mrs. Pillsbury told him when he was twelve years old.

4. (*Black*) Cynthia was taught *Pro Vita Sua* in her Catholic high school and was a member of an anti- abortion club. Attended a protest against *Roe v. Wade* during her senior year of high school.

5. (*White*) Bill rejects his own faith in the first year at university, his first time away from home, and never again has a religious affiliation.

5. (*Black*) Practices contraception in her second year at her university, still goes to church, and receives communion.

6. (*White*) RESIGNS

It is not impossible or improbable for a player to be at a disadvantage before the opponent has been named or met. Likewise, *White*'s chance of winning this match decreased catastrophically when Black opened her game. White's aimlessness by move **5.** combined with Black's beautifully consistent inconsistency in following her faith and principles made Larkin insuperable.

MATCH SCORE Pillsbury 4 – 4 – 3   Larkin 4 – 4 – 3

Games 12 and 13

Game 12
The Car Game (1980 - 1995)

Very few "Car Games" do not start with hand-me-downs, casting the parents' shadows over the first part of the game. In both Bill and Cynthia's adolescence, the moves feature GM and Ford vehicles. Although by mid-game, there's hardly an American car nor even a truck or Jeep in sight. The advantage of the behemoth American models that Cynthia's father bought, directly resulted in his having sexual experiences in the back seat. Cynthia didn't know that, like Elaine Robinson in *The Graduate*, she was conceived in the back seat of a Ford (two weeks before the impatient Larkins were married). Cynthia didn't like cars, in general, and specifically hated driving them, getting them serviced, and putting in the gasoline herself. As a social requisite, **6. She took the driver's test and passed after the third attempt when she was seventeen.** But **7. She usually let her girlfriends drive her everywhere.** Her parents didn't hand her a car *per se*. She was given a Chevy Impala in which her uncle had died of a heart attack outside his physician's office. It took time to forget what happened inside the vehicle but, luckily, her relationship with Bill minimized her need to drive it. **8...Bill called the Impala the Death-mobile.** Their first scrape over cars occurred in the first year of marriage when one or the other couldn't find car keys (see Game 1). By this time, **14. Cynthia bought her first foreign brand, Nissan, and she has stuck with the company since.** Why not? **19. Her Nissans were recalled only twice: once for the brakes and, then, for a faulty passenger airbag.** She became diligent taking care of her car once she bought it herself. **22. She got a strange satisfaction getting the 3000 mile oil change. 22...Bill kept telling her than she could've waited longer; the 3000 mile checkup was the way car dealers made extra money on naive drivers.** Similarly, she regularly got new transmission fluid; constantly checked the air in her tires; and bought new tires after 30000 miles. She rarely had a breakdown far from her home. Whereas, nothing inhibited Bill's ability to gain an advantage than his having constant breakdowns. He had also moved on to a Japanese company, a Toyota truck, which **16...He inherited from the landscaping business.** Seemed such a bargain. NOT! **17. "You've spent more money repairing that piece of junk than I paid for a new car."** Was it the manufacturer's incompetence, which Bill often cited, or his own complacency toward western civilization's most complex invention for everyday use? Did his incessant purchasing of used cars and trucks prevent him from developing a better relationship with his vehicle, as one would do with a newborn son or daughter, ultimately prevent his attaining victory in a game where, historically, most men prevailed? Women, like Cynthia, often experienced dealership intimidation, like being pressured to take extra warranties and insisting a tire with a slow leak be replaced instead of plugging it. This was where Cynthia was strong but not necessarily imaginative. She would research every move she would make involving automobiles, much to Bill's amusement, and went so far that **24. She took a male friend, not Bill, a fellow teacher, to the Nissan showroom who coached her to haggle for a better price** which resulted in **25. Cynthia leaving the dealership only moments before she was to sign the contract.** Meanwhile, **28. Bill bought a Ram truck 4 x 4, used, the kind of truck he had wanted for ten years.** Bill's biggest issue in the game occurred when **23. Bill drives Cynthia's car through high water** and **...23. "The car hasn't driven right since that bad storm."** What wouldn't suffice was **24. He doesn't acknowledge that anything was wrong** or **24. No water went into the tailpipe.** Instead, **24...He asks her to wait a few more months before deciding on a new car.** He figured the car was nearly five years old and Cynthia would probably buy a new model. He didn't expect **25. "I liked the way the car talked to me when I didn't buckle my seat belt."** This and other aural features would not appear in future Maxima models. Cynthia's game lost momentum when she bought her next car and decided to lease it for five years and then buy it. **27..."Why not buy it outright?"** She didn't see how she would be paying more in the long run.

He thought she knew cars. Did the guy who was coaching her on how to negotiate with a car salesman advise this? Was she listening to the salesman because she liked him a lot? Bill's fleeting thought of Cynthia's potential infidelity quickly receded because of the distraction caused by Tara's projectile vomiting! In one area, Bill couldn't keep up with her. Cynthia earned 8 speeding tickets between 1991 and 1994. For one so reluctant to start driving as a teenager, she threw herself into the game and held her position against what was supposed to be an easy male victory. DRAW.

MATCH SCORE Pillsbury 4 – 4 – 4   Larkin 4 – 4 – 4

Game 13

The Movie Game (1972 - 1992)

Another game in which parents dictated the opening moves but failed to make a lasting-impression on their kids. Cynthia went to the movies with her girlfriends and parents. Cynthia's choices in movies were inconsistent. First, it was things her parents wanted her to see, like *The Parent Trap* with Hayley Mills when Cynthia was seven. Then *Sleeping Beauty*, the witch scaring her for months. Bill followed the same pattern to the point that he was seeing mostly the same movies as Cynthia. Nowhere else in this game would their predilections be in sync. Bill was taken to *Lilies of the Field*, which bored him, but the second film of this double feature was *Palm Springs Weekend*, which starred many actors from his favrorite television shows, capped by the presence of his fantasy sweetheart from *Hawaiian Eye*, Connie Stevens. On her own...4 **Cynthia liked popular, largely non-violent fare: *Mary Poppins*, *The Sound of Music*, and others.** She disdained Frankie Avalon and Annette Funicello beach movies, just as Bill had done despite having once had a crush on Annette. However, Bill could be found **5. watching on television American International pictures, like *The Wild Angels*, *Hell's Angels in Vietnam*, and *Masque of the Red Death*, and any other Vincent Price horror film, films beneath dignity for Cynthia.** Bill and Cynthia have different tastes in movies, but as a couple – and they aren't alone in this

– they believe part of their mutual attraction and love make these differences irrelevant. Their romanticized enthusiasm sufficiently represses the reality that their shared experiences are an artificial means to do things together. All that then matters is for one player to force a quaint psychological struggle for. . .for not quite anything they could define for themselves. She was the first to stir the movie pot with a move initiated in ...6: **"We always see the movies you want to see?" 7. He thought she said she wanted to see** *Police Academy.* **...7. "It was your type of movie." 8. "Why don't you go to the movies you like by yourself?"** A couple years later Bill emphatically told Cynthia that he didn't think much of a movie that both had, beforehand, seemed interested in seeing: *Broadcast News.* **10. "I didn't think Holly Hunter was that attractive or compelling as a news person. ...10. "So says the specialist on television broadcasting."** They didn't think much of these remarks, nor did their next several movie choices create caustic comments, although Cynthia had wanted to say how stupid *Die Hard* was. The lack of any comments after the fact may have built up emotions that would result in an unexpected move. Snarky commentary occurred intermittently the next couple years until the first pregnancy. Cynthia was keen on seeing *Dead Poets Society*, but a week before they would be having their movie night (usually every other Saturday), Bill told her he didn't feel like seeing it. Cynthia was surprised, as someone is surprised when she no longer has her way. Not that she had her way with many of the movies they saw together. It was as if they "mutually had their way." Why didn't he want to see it? **12. Bill refuses to go with Cynthia to see** *Dead Poets Society*. Cynthia offered a modicum resistance. **12..."I've waited for months. All the teachers at school loved it. 13. This was exactly why Bill didn't want to go. 13..."I'm seeing it regardless."** Her insistence was a first. What made it worse, it would now be a week and a half before she could now see the movie. They looked back at this episode as their "first fight". They were married but Emily wouldn't be born until six months later. **15. "There's five other movies we could see." 15..."I don't see why you're resisting so much."** For the first time, at least tangibly, "having one's way" became important for them. **16. "I'm not a big Robin Williams fan."** Bill's reasoning veered toward the ridiculous **16..."You watched** *Mork and Mindy*.**" 17. "I didn't really like it."** But they had watched the television show together. For a moment, it registered for her that their reason for doing things together was not as natural as it seemed. **18. "You can see it with your teacher friends."** Cynthia did just this, and Bill's move wasn't bad considering that saw the real reason that he didn't want to go. It's not as if he expected her to come with him to *Lawnmower Man*. They didn't stop going to the movies together but they started going to separate movies. The distinguishing break again was Bill's suggestion **24. They went to the same multiplex but saw different shows.** They could manage this at mega complexes with 16 to 24 theaters where they would be sure their respective movies started and ended within fifteen minutes of the other. Watching movies at home proved to be simpler and without much comment or enmity once they bought a second television. Bill usually watched his films in the bedroom unless he wanted to catch one after midnight. Hence, the game barely reached endgame before they lived in separate houses. DRAW.

MATCH SCORE: Pillsbury 4 – 4 – 5   Larkin 4 – 4 – 5

The Political Game

A struggle in which no one wins, no one loses, no one gives in. There are perhaps more brilliant moves in this game than in any other. Some have called this the "Exclamation Point" Game. It could also be called the Eternal Game, having started before they met and continued after they divorced. Actually, someone loses!

Larkin: *White*   Pillsbury: *Black*

1. (*White*) If she could have voted (she was 17 and a half) in the 1980 election, Cynthia would have chosen President Carter for another term.

1. (*Black*) He never liked Jimmy Carter, especially after Carter made the comment in *Playboy* about lusting after women in his heart. What was so goddamn wrong with that?.

Some may have wanted an (!) beside *Black*'s first move, just as twice as many critics of the Match wanted a (?) beside *White*'s first move. It should be remembered that Black was skeptical about beginning this game with **"Ronald Reagan would make a great President."** Those who want to give an (!) to *Black*, or even to *White*, well before Carter received the Nobel Peace Prize in 2002, might have forgotten that the candidates themselves were not openly embraced and many felt that Carter and Reagan represented no choice for the electorate. Neither considered John Anderson seriously.

2. (*White*) "Carter told the people they were being selfish," she rationalized later. "It might not have been smart politically, but he was always honest. His Human Rights campaign is something Americans can be proud of for many generations."

2. (*Black*) "America has never been less respected around the world than during Carter's presidency. Giving away the Panama Canal. The Ayatollah returned the hostages as soon as Reagan became President. Khomeini was afraid of what Reagan might do to Iran."

3. (*White*) "His own Vice-President called Reagan's low taxes - more defense spending plan 'Voodoo Economics.'"

3. (*Black*) "Seventeen percent inflation. Ten percent unemployment. Your boy and the Democrats drove this country into the ground."

4. (*White*) "You never said that you liked Reagan."

4. (*Black*) "He brought America back to respectability." (!)

The key aspect of Pillsbury's's move, the first great move of the game, shows that his commitment to the Democrats and the Republicans is contingent upon their respective strengths. He will not be swayed by arguments or advertisements. In fact, in the recesses of Bill's voting are the potential moves: **"I don't give a fuck," "politics is shit,"** and **"It doesn't matter who wins."** Now the importance of their first moves is revealed. They are split politically and never will find agreement. Had they never voted, we might not even have seen their expertise displayed in this area. Almost as good for *Black* would have been 4...**"Are you better off than you were four years ago?"**

5. (*White*) Reagan fired the air traffic controllers and endangered all passenger flights in the U.S.
5. (*Black*) The air traffic controllers were federal employees and not allowed to strike.

6. (*White*) "When did you ever care for the law?"

Better **6. I thought you were a union man.** *Black* probably would not be able to resist a dissipation of energy by replying: **6...."I've never belonged to a union my whole life."** And then *White* could have answered 7. **"Your father was. His father was. I've never heard you say anything good about business people."** And *Black* would have further mired himself with 7...**"I think it's ridiculous for teachers to form unions."**

6. (*Black*) Reagan was nearly killed in an assassination attempt.

7. (*White*) One would have thought that would have made him support gun-control legislation.

7. (*Black*) The assassination and the whole sacking of the air controllers gained Reagan enough support around the country to pass his tax cuts and defense increases.

8. (*White*) David Stockman's article in *The Atlantic*.

This move should have halted *Black*'s momentum and provided *White* with an (!). All onlookers, professional and amateur, assumed it would.

8. (*Black*) What did people care about the inner workings of the administration? Yes, it was embarrassing. But Reagan's toned down inflation. The Carter economic nightmare was over.

9. (*White*) Reagan produced the worst recession since the Great Depression.

9. (*Black*) The Equal Rights Amendment will not pass, even with a seven year extension. (!)

The genius of *Black*'s move could be examined for several pages. First, he turns from the bad economic news to one of the great conservative triumphs of the decade. No, the anti-Amendment sentiment was not great, just enough in a few key states. And should *White* have responded:
10. Phyllis Schlafly launched a campaign of fear and

misinformation about the ERA to stop it, *Black* could have moved **10...Women are already protected under the Constitution and the 1964 Civil Rights Act,** and bogged her down with valid information but a kind that proves superfluous to the issues brought to the fore by the ERA. Yet, it is the secondary assault of the move, the personal way *White* took the defeat of the amendment.

10. (*White*) Two hundred and forty-one Marines were killed in a suicide attack in Beirut, Lebanon.
10. (*Black*) The invasion of Grenada drove out a Communist regime.

11. (*White*) "El Salvador is about to become a new Vietnam," she worried.
11. (*Black*) The Contras in Nicaragua are freedom fighters worthy of the respect our nation gives to our own freedom fighters of 1776.

12. (*White*) Archbishop Romero assassinated.
12. (*Black*) The Soviet Union declared the Evil Empire.

13. (*White*) The Boland Amendment prevented aid to be used to overthrow the government of Nicaragua.   (?)

White's aggressiveness comes a little late. Weak argumentation in terms of getting public support. *Black* does not return fire with **13...The Reagan administration** interpreted the Boland amendment as applying to the intelligence agencies and let the National Security Agency handle the funding of the Contras. Although *White* could offer the plausible countermeasure: **14. Why did Poindexter and North handle the funding secretly?** The public did not care about constitutional technicalities.

13. (*Black*) The economy's getting better every day. The Dow Jones just passed 1000.

14. (*White*) The "sleaze factor" clings to many Reagan appointments including the Cabinet, with the likes of Ray Donovan and Ed Meese, and lower level appointees, many of whom were indicted for influence peddling.
14. (*Black*) "Are we better off than we were four years ago?" he asks Cynthia but doesn't wait for her answer.

The election of 1984 was so deeply in the bag that Pillsbury did not bother to vote.

15. (*White*) Reagan visited the graves of the Nazi S.S. soldiers.
15. (*Black*) "The media distorts everything he does. The President was honoring all the soldiers killed in the D-Day fighting."

16. (*White*) Nancy Reagan consulted an astrologer and determines her husband's schedule according to the

alignment of the stars.

16. (*Black*) "*You* consult the astrology page once in a while."

17. (*White*) "I don't run the country. It proves he's manipulated not just by her but by his advisers. He doesn't have a thought of his own."

White summed up very well the general opinion of her fellow Democrats. It also looks like the right move to make. Its relative ineffectiveness will always bug *White*'s fans, who seem never to have understood that what made Reagan popular was the reason that they hated him so much. The same will be true later in the game, perhaps not for exactly the same reason, when *Black*'s moves during the Clinton years do not have the effect *Black*'s fans thought they should have. The alternative 17. "**He understands the governing function of the Presidency**" seems so distasteful and, worse, could provide *Black* with the future countermove in a critical situation: "**Didn't you admit, once, Reagan knew what he was doing?**"

17. (*Black*) Reagan meets Gorbachev at Reykjavik.

18. (*White*) The Iran-Contra Scandal.
18. (*Black*) Bill wears an "Ollie North for President" tee shirt.

19. (*White*) Admiral Poindexter, North, and others are indicted; the Secretary of Defense and Vice-President are under suspicion.

19. (*Black*) Ninety-million dollars spent by the Special Prosecutor and no convictions. Republicans call for the diminishing of the Special Prosecutor's powers.

Republicans did not get what they wanted, which allowed them to get what they wanted in the future. Does this make *Black*'s last move good or bad? Some expert commentary escapes the expert's expertise.

20. (*White*) The Stock Market Crashes. Wall Street Closes for a few days.

20. (*Black*) The Pillsbury-Larkin family portfolio remains relatively untouched.

Better than the abstract **20...More people became billionaires in the 1980s than in all the previous decades in the history of the world.** *Black* knew that the family mattered most, although the move hinged on the favorable circumstance that Bill's broker did not gamble with his clients' life savings.

21. (*White*) *These men were not weak men, but they permitted themselves to grow short-sighted and selfish; and while many of them down at the bottom possessed the fundamental virtues, including the fighting virtues, others were purely of*

the glorified huckster or glorified pawnbroker type--which when developed to the exclusion of everything else makes about as poor a national type as the world has seen. -- Teddy Roosevelt, *Autobiography* [Cynthia found the quote in an old paperback book at a library discard sale, *Eight Essays* by Edmund Wilson.]

21. (Black) *We need true tax reform that will at least make a start toward restoring for our children the American Dream that wealth is denied no one, that each individual has the right to fly as high as his strength and ability will take him....But we can not have such reform while our tax policy is engineered by people who view the tax as a means of achieving change in our social structure....* -- Ronald Reagan, "The Time for Choosing" speech, 1964

22. (White) *"I believe in state's rights and I believe in fighting the Russians with the most doing people as much as they can for themselves at the community level and at the private level. I believe we have distorted the balance of government today by giving powers that never were intended to be given in the Constitution to that federal establishment."* [Reagan speech in Philadelphia, Mississippi, 1980.]

Using a politician's words against himself can prove bountiful; however, using those same words against a supporter of that same politician, even a tepid supporter like Bill, might not produce the desired defensive tizzy.

22. (*Black*) Russians pull out of Afghanistan, after fifty thousand dead, their nine years there come to be called "their Vietnam."

23. (*White*) After the Democratic convention, Dukakis leads Vice-President Bush by ten to twenty percent in the polls.
23. (*Black*) Michael Dukakis is a card-carrying member of the ACLU.

24. (*White*) Garry Trudeau represents Bush as the invisible man in *Doonesbury.*   (?)

So pleasing, so gratifying to the *Doonesbury* readers. The feeling that the entire country feels the same about the Republican candidate will be belied by the November polls. White does not realize how her contempt for Reagan, Bush, and the Republican conservative agenda would leak into her respect for her husband as a marriage-chess player. She could not understand how Black's candidates could win when Pillsbury had nothing near her passion for politics and the results of the presidential elections. Long gone are the Pillsbury - Hutton, Larkin - Walsh days when the wives seemingly voted the husbands' way. Larkin's dad fervently wanted Stevenson over Eisenhower because Nixon was running as Vice-President. Walsh had secret fantasies about Nixon which may explain her propensity for paranoid reconstructions of events. Indeed,

Larkin's game against Walsh suffered when he realized fully the extent of his dislike for Walsh and, ultimately, caused his defeat.

24. (*Black*) The Willie Horton and Boston Harbor ads.

25. (*White*) George Bush cannot avoid the "wimp factor" despite being a Navy pilot during World War II.
25. (*Black*) Democrats refuse to counter Bush attack ads or confront the Republican accusation that Dukakis is the "L" word.

26. (*White*) "I knew Jack Kennedy and *you* are no Jack Kennedy."

Too little too late. Few experts can explain why nothing *White* tried worked. Even fewer gave her little chance to win the game at this point. What *White* could have responded 24. **"There is nothing wrong with standing up for the rights of reprehensible individuals because the strength of our Constitution lies in its application to all people at any time."** Likewise, in response to *Black*'s reckless attack on the 24th move, *White* could have countered with 25. **The death penalty is a shortsighted solution to violent crimes in our society** or some other rationalization in response to the theoretical question posed by CNN journalist Bernard Shaw at the start of one of the debates.

26. (*Black*) Berlin Wall comes down and many communist nations in Eastern Europe force out their communist regimes.

27. (*White*) "Burning the flag" and "anti-abortion" amendments to the Constitution do not pass through Congress.

Why do we have the sense that the game is on auto-pilot?

27. (*Black*) Invasion of Panama and the surrender of Manuel Noreiga to American custody as the rightful leader is elevated to the Presidency.

28. (*White*) Almost all Latin American nations protest the U. S. invasion, while many people in the United States wonder about Noreiga's affiliation with the CIA.
28. (*Black*) Iraq invades Kuwait, and President Bush virtually alone calls for intervention: "This will not stand." (!)

29. (*White*) Democrats call for sanctions and many experts fear a prolonged war and heavy casualties, invoking the specter of the war in Vietnam.(?)
29. (*Black*) Bush, Cheney, Scowcroft, and Rumsfeld secure a multi-nation coalition, including Syria, and launch Operation Desert Storm and what is called the 100-Hour War.

30. (*White*) Saddam Hussein is not removed from power.

After the "**100-Hour War**" move, it seemed as if the pit could not be any deeper for *White*. There could be no way for her to salvage respectability. There had been neither resolution in her moves since **18** and **19**, the Iran-Contra gambit, nor anything resembling a strategy save for fighting on her heels. The Dukakis re-positioning, we understand, was not the first option; however, when the Gary Hart thrusts never materialized, she could have shown greater enthusiasm and guts. **White** would learn from these mistakes, but it begs the question: why must players reach the abyss before they can know the right move? Fortunately, *White* had help. The overwhelming approval ratings for Bush bred *Black*'s overconfidence, which meant underestimating what the American electorate really worries about. Perhaps Saddam's own escape from the abyss did not affect *Black*'s future moves, but it would be foolish to think that his death would not have greatly helped seal the game.

30. (Black) George Bush registers the highest approval rating for a President since the poll has been taken.

31. (*White*) Bill Clinton gains the Democratic nomination despite several setbacks, most notably the Jennifer Flowers scandal, although he seems to have created real enthusiasm within the Democratic Party. Cynthia defends

him against the womanizing charges.

31. (*Black*) The Bush re-election campaign aims at Clinton's lack of military service, his attempt to use Senatorial influence to avoid the draft, his lame story about smoking a joint, and his joining a protest in England against the Vietnam War.

32. (*White*) "It's the economy, stupid." (!)
32. (*Black*) Bill votes for Perot. (!)

A great move followed by one's opponent's best move. Could Trudeau's "invisible President" hold the basic truth of that President's fall from power? Namely, the man inspired no loyalty because few truly believed he was his own man. Revenge of the Wimp Factor!! What *White* did not factor in was *Black*'s ability to recognize a stagnant presidency. Bill read *Doonesbury*!! But not even in the voting booth will Black descend to the depths and pull a Democratic lever. In the latter stages of his parents' Match, Pillsbury - Hutton, Pillsbury deviated from his lifelong straight Democratic voting to vote for Nixon against McGovern. Hearing his Dad's confession over this must have made a lasting impression on Bill.

33. (*White*) Despite having trouble mobilizing his Presidency, Clinton creates initiatives in domestic policy not seen since the late 1970s.
33. (*Black*) The Vince Foster suicide, the Paula Jones

harassment suit, and the dogged attacks by conservative media critics.

After *White*'s weak move at **33**, *Black* responds with a ferocity not seen since the political games of the McCarthy Era. Capturing the King does not seem enough, only annihilation of *White*'s political beachhead will do. Some commentators believe this game perfectly reflects the overall relationship between Cynthia and Bill because, in the 1990s, their relationship devolved to the most bitter of contests: the post-divorce potshots. *White*'s mistakes early in the game were due to her inability to understand and appreciate Ronald Reagan's abilities. Now *Black* echoes these errors when conservatives couldn't understand why everyone did not see the Bill Clinton that they saw. At least, *Black* will show more creativity, however superficial, in his next response to a relatively weak move.

34. (*White*) Hillary Clinton became the most politically involved First Lady since Eleanor Roosevelt.
34. (*Black*) The Contract with America and Newt Gingrich's ascension to Speaker of the House during the off year elections stymied Clinton's first term.

35. (*White*) Clinton hired Dick Morris as a consultant to manage his comeback after flirting with political extinction and won a relatively easy victory to gain a second term.

An ugly, ugly move from all perspectives. Instead of playing for outright victory after making the greatest comeback in any of the games of this Match thus far, *White* plays a game of attrition when she has a decided disadvantage in manpower. *White* is flush with the prospect of winning the game in the wake of a resounding victory over Bob Dole, an absolute overestimation of the power of winning. Did the Democrats not know that Bob Dole was NOT Richard Nixon or even Gerald Ford? Nor will the Republicans stop pressuring President Clinton after the adrenaline rushes of potential scandals within the Oval Office itself. Even to the point of nearly kidding themselves that Clinton could be removed from office before his term is up. The remainder of this game tests which side's illusions will outlast the other's.

35 (*Black*) Continuing Whitewater investigation and the appointment of a Special Prosecutor, Kenneth Starr, hunt for wrongdoings before and during the Clinton Presidency.

36. (*White*) The deficit is reduced to two trillion dollars; meanwhile, Wall Street continues the longest Bull Market in history.

36. (*Black*) The Paula Jones case is renewed: Ms. Jones retains new lawyers, paid for by a conservative think tank, and Bill Clinton testifies on videotape for the grand jury.

37. (*White*) Moderately successful interventions in Haiti and Bosnia.

37. (*Black*) Monica Lewinsky does not take her blue dress to the cleaners, then calls up a friend to ask for advice.

38. (*White*) Serbian forces eventually leave Kosovo; Milosevich leaves power in Serbia and will be tried for war crimes.

38. (*Black*) "I never had sexual relations with that woman, Ms. Lewinsky."   (!)

Just as good: **38...**"**It depends on what the definition of 'is' is.**" Again, nothing beats the use of one's opponent's words against one's opponent.

39. (*White*) The Clinton administration works hard to negotiate agreements between Catholics and Protestants in Northern Ireland and between Jews and Palestinians in Israel.

White believes Clinton's legacy will start from these maneuvers and obscure all scandals and legislative failures.

39. (*Black*) The House of Representatives impeaches President Clinton.

40. (*White*) The Senate acquits President Clinton.

40. (*Black*) "This is a campaign about character," Bill informed his new wife.

Black's move is a variation of its gambit in **31**. Why it works here, more strikingly works against a different candidate, might perplex the amateur. Remember, fewer pieces are on the board and *White* has clearly lost momentum.

41. (*White*) Cynthia campaigns for ex-Senator Bill Bradley despite not caring that he was once an All-American Basketball player and a leader on two NBA championships for the New York Knicks.
41. (*Black*) Bill likes John McCain because he was a prisoner during the Vietnam War and an American hero.

42. (*White*) Al Gore defeats Bradley on Super Tuesday; Cynthia joins the Gore campaign in June.
42. (*Black*) McCain wins the New Hampshire primary, but George W. Bush wins all the primaries on Super Tuesday.

Pillsbury wins by his candidate losing.

43. (*White*) Gore wins Florida.

This move seemed to have given White a victory.

43. (*Black*) *Fox News* declares Bush the winner.   (!)

44. (*White*) Gore cuts Bush's lead in Florida to two hundred votes.

44. (*Black*) Bush sends James Baker to Florida to prevent a Democratic victory.

This move insures that *Black* will not lose unless, although it would not definitely spell victory, *White* decided **46. Democrats immediately ask for a recount for the entire state of Florida** would not be enough.

45. (*White*) Gore campaign fights for and win from the State Supreme Court the right to recount votes in Dade County.

45. (*Black*) Supreme Court asks the Florida State Court to reconsider its decision.

46. (*White*) RESIGNS

Black's superlative **43th** move forced *White* into an inferior position out of which it could not claw.

MATCH SCORE: Pillsbury 5 – 4 – 5   Larkin 4 – 5 – 5

Pillsbury only needs one more win. It could come at any time. However, the reader well knows there are 20 games. The fact that the Match reached 20 games must mean the 20th was the final one. It also means that Larkin can still win. But we will also see how close each player came to taking it all. One bad move in the one of the remaining six games might make the difference.

Game 15

The "Music" game

Just barely a game. Before they met, Bill listened to AM and FM rock stations and had an eclectic album collection: the Beatles' White Album, Jimi Hendrix Experience's Electric Ladyland, and the Who's rock opera Tommy were his favorites and he managed to keep the vinyl albums despite many years passing and many housing moves. He bought 45s occasionally which he carelessly looked after, as was the case with his cassettes. At some point, after marrying Cynthia, he listened more and more to Country Music, culminating in his watching the Country Music Awards. He liked the personalities old and new: Hank Williams, Johnny Cash, Tammy Wynette, Patsy Cline, Loretta Lynn. ...8. **Cynthia attributes his new taste in music to Bill's watching *The Beverly Hillbillies* reruns.** She shared her early tastes with Bill and, like him, shifted from her favorite rock groups: The Eagles, ELO, Journey, and Neil Young. She clung to the earlier sounds of Motown: The Supremes, Miracles, Temptations, and Marvin Gaye, and always had time to listen to the Beach Boys. But there was always a latent interest in classical music, emblematic with high culture, and her periods of listening to it coincided with difficult times with Bill, especially after the birth of Tara. DRAW.

MATCH SCORE Pillsbury 5 – 4 – 6   Larkin 4 – 5 – 6

GAME 16 (1990-1992)

CUTE BABY GAME II

A game that leaves the commentator speechless.

Larkin *White*   Pillsbury *Black*

1. (*White*) "Do you want to have a sister, Emily?"
1. (*Black*) "Wouldn't you like to have a brother, Em?"

2. (*White*) "She told me she doesn't want to share Mommy and Daddy with anyone else."
2. (*Black*) "She needs to have another kid around. You see what happens to only children at school. Spoiled and narcissistic."

3. (*White*) "We shouldn't have another baby right away. Wait a few years when we have the money."
3. (*Black*) "We'll never be more energetic," Bill replies. "Money won't be a problem as long as we love them."

4. (*White*) She is worried about her job, taking another leave so soon, just two years after having Emily.
4. (*Black*) He wants her to give up teaching, eventually.

5. (*White*) "You can't ask me to stay home day after day. I have a Masters degree."
5. (*Black*) "I meant until both kids are in school."

6. (*White*) "You'll probably want another one after that. I won't have the energy to revitalize my career when I am forty-five years old."
6. (*Black*) "You promised after having Emily that we would have another child."

7. (*White*) "It was never a promise. I think, more than ever, we should wait. We have to be sure we will be together."
7. (*Black*) "We're only seeing a counselor. It doesn't mean we're splitting up, now or later. Everyone's been wondering when Emily is going to have a playmate."

8. (*White*) "Don't give me your 'everyone's been wondering' shit again. That's the worst reason in the world to get pregnant."
8. (*Black*) "I'll tell you what's bullshit. Putting your career before raising your children."

9. (*White*) "Don't raise your voice, Emily will wake up. She'll sense something's up."
9. (*Black*) "What's bullshit about 'everyone wondering'?" he asks in a low voice.

10. (*White*) "'Everyone' is your frickin' mother. I'm sick of her insinuating herself into every nook and cranny of our marriage."
10. (*Black*) "My mother likes being a grandmother. Unlike your psycho mother who is oblivious to not only mine but

her own daughter's desires."

11. (*White*) "You think a baby will fix our relationship."
11. (*Black*) "I love you more now than I ever have."

12. (*White*) "You don't want to admit there's a problem. That's your problem."
12. (*Black*) "Because Suzanne Gallagher had a thing for me, that constitutes a crisis."

13. (*White*) "This is the only time we talk, when we're discussing the state of our relationship."
13. (*Black*) "I'm trying to understand what you want."

14. (*White*) "You were the one who was so upset when I first got pregnant. Only a guy could be eager for more pregnancies."
14. (*Black*) "You could try a cesarean and have your tubes tied later. That way you could never accuse me of pressuring you to have another."

15. (*White*) "I want you to stop pressuring me *now*."
15. (*Black*) "What pressure? I'm thinking about our family's future and Emily's happiness."

16. (*White*) "Now you are using Emily to coerce me. That's as low as you can get."
16. (*Black*) "We can't base a decision on what we think

Emily wants. It is what is best for her."

17. (*White*) "How could you let this happen? What are you thinking? The pill isn't foolproof. You know that."
17. (*Black*) "So I didn't use protection. It's not the first time."

18. (*White*) "I want an abortion."
18. (*Black*) "You can't do this to...us. Life is something sacred. You'll be hurting everyone who loves you. You'll be hurting yourself. At least ask our counselor what you should do."

19. (*White*) "She said it was my decision."
19. (*Black*) "But she advised against it."

20. (*White*) "'Advice' is all it was. I don't know what to do."
20. (*Black*) "She said to consider it a new start. You want this marriage to work out, don't you? Would you really leave me?"

21. (*White*) "I want another girl."
21. (*Black*) "I want to name this one. Tara if it's a girl. Jeffrey if we get a boy."

22. (*White*) She had no objection nor did she offer a comment or compliment.
22. (*Black*) "Emily' will be happy she's going to have someone to boss around."

23. (*White*) "I want to kill myself every time I get morning sickness."

23. (*Black*) "I wish we had saved the bassinet and changing table."

24. (White) "It was your idea to sell it. We didn't have room in the row house. Obviously, you weren't looking ahead for the family's welfare then."

24. (Black) "You didn't stop me."

25. (*White*) "Tara's been throwing up whenever I breast feed her."

25. (*Black*) "Give her the other milk."

26. (*White*) "So now you're a doctor. She can't keep anything down."

26. (*Black*) "She might have lactose intolerance. At least our insurance covers this."

27. (*White*) "The doctors don't know why she's doing it."

27. (*Black*) "I can't believe it. I'm calling that quack."

28. (*White*) "If you had gone there with me...."

28. (*Black*) "Tara can't gain weight."

29. (*White*) "Do you want to take her to another doctor? He'll say the same as the others."

29. (*Black*) "I didn't realize a baby could have this kind of

strength," Bill says, wiping the projectile vomiting from the kitchen wall.

30. (*White*) "You're the one who wanted another mouth to feed."
30. (*Black*) "How come it took the doctors so long to figure out it was an esophagus problem?"

31. (*White*) Cynthia smacks Emily after the girl had tried to push her sister down the stairs.
31. (*Black*) "Mommy hit me, Daddy."

32. (*White*) "She has to know how dangerous pushing is."
32. (*Black*) "We agreed we would never hit them."

33. (*White*) "That was before we had two of them."
33. (*Black*) "You wanted a divorce all along. You don't even try to talk to me civilly, not even when the girls are in front of us."

34. (*White*) "I'm going back to teaching in September. We will have to hire someone to come over or take Tara to day care."
34. (*Black*) "You can't trust others to raise your kids. I'll stay home if I have to."

35. (*White*) She drops Tara off in the morning and picks up Emily in the afternoon.

35. (*Black*) He drops Emily off at school and picks up Tara around four in the afternoon.

36. (*White*) She tells her friend, Clara, that Tara's sickness began the worst part of her life. They were helpless to do anything. The house took on an odor. She lost her desire for any sex during this period. She made Bill think it was the aftermath of the surgery to tie her tubes. Tara's throwing up seemed to be her own ejection of Bill from her system.

36. (*Black*) "We might ask my mother to come over once or twice a week. Until I get the new franchise."

37. (*White*) "It doesn't have anything to do with sex, you asshole. It's you. Your fucking primitive conception of what this family is. You just want to spin around the house and take photographs of every move they make. You used a whole role of film with Tara puking her tiny insides out."

Stalemate

MATCH SCORE Pillsbury 5 – 4 – 5 – 1
                      Larkin 4 – 5 – 5 – 1

The Hold the Mayo Game

There may have been no winner or loser in this game but the action embodies the emotional end of their marriage. It only takes a small, irrelevant episode, one not recorded anywhere, least of all in the players' memories, to push them to major decisions and actions, regardless who will be hurt.

Pillsbury *White*   Larkin   *Black*

1. (*White*) "We don't have much in the fridge, hon."
1. (*Black*) Cynthia says nothing and looks for herself. She finds a can of Bumble Bee Solid White Albacore (in water).

The depth of the psychological-magma is waiting to come to the surface after their tectonic plates become more unaligned. *White*'s opening comment suggests that the last person who shopped for groceries – he assumed it was her – inadequately supplied the family with enough food. More poignantly, they had been talking before lunch about *Black*'s last supermarket visit, where she had run into Fran Clifton, creating an uncomfortable few minutes. Bill had hoped to find lunch meat, ham or turkey and Swiss cheese, perhaps Lebanon bologna. If this weren't enough, the refrigerator was filled with dinner leftovers, five kinds of juices, two loaves of bread, half a bag of hot dog rolls but no frankfurters in the lunch meat drawer, and many types of probiotic yogurt. Lest you believe Cynthia was taking too much shit from her husband's bland observation, and the commentator's sharp and exhaustive exegesis, examine her mental shotgun blast back in her husband's direction. First, she doesn't verbally respond but brushes by him and looks for herself, as if she didn't know what was in there, knowing her cursory glance was buying time for her to suggest an irritating comeback. And she succeeded. The can of albacore tuna had been partially hidden on the middle shelf in the back, conservatively estimated to be there many months, though the sales expiration date was still long in coming. Did she know that he had bought the tuna, originally? No matter, since the game took an unexpected turn with Bill's *ad hoc* gambit. A final note: unlike most of the games, this one offers little or no opportunity to suggest alternative moves or strategies, as in speed chess.

2. (*White*) "Do we have any bagels?"
2. (*Black*) "Tuna on bagels? I was thinking English muffins or croissants."

3. (*White*) "We have croissants! Great."

One could almost imagine the emotional landscape smoothing out the jagged mountains into some rolling hills.

3. (*Black*) "Actually, we don't have any croissants," she smirked.

4. (*White*) "Why'd you mention them?"
4. (*Black*) She explained that hers were potential choices. But they did have muffins.

5. (*White*) He never liked English muffins, which he thought were an unappetizing example of a pretentiously named breakfast bun.

In other words, fuck the nook and crannies bullshit. The English muffin, to him, had increasingly represented an aspect of Cynthia's character and taste that he couldn't respect anymore. Obviously, the English muffin became one of many things in her diet and fashion palate that caused a twinge in his thoughts about her.

5. (*Black*) "We could just do them on bread," she said, pulling out the 15 Grain whole wheat, the Rye and Pumpernickel Deli Swirl, and the seedless Rye.

Not a great deal of proper meal planning or pantry stocking for this couple. At this point in the Match, a.k.a. their married life, structures within the household disappeared or were in the state of collapse. Other examples: dirty dishes in the sink and clothes left in the dryer for several days.

6. (*White*) Still miffed by the "croissant" move, he nixes the bread idea.

6. (*Black*) "Rye Pump is one of your favorites," Cynthia comments tersely.

Pillsbury cannot give in, even if it puts himself in a bad position later on. His rationalization for not eating bread is not so slightly nullified by his overall strategy in the "You Are What You Eat" game.

7. (*White*) "I'll just do a salad with lettuce and tomato. Cut down on the carbs."

7. (*Black*) She finds one tomato, large but slightly overripe.

At an earlier stage of their marriage, they would've ordered a pizza. And Bill wouldn't have made a peep about Carbs.

8. (*White*) "We can use it."

8. (Black) "Weren't you going to stop at the Produce Junction, yesterday?"

9. (*White*) "It was out of the way coming home."

9. (*Black*) "At least we have Swiss cheese."

The point of Black's move being that she bought a half-pound of Finlandia three days before. AND she went out of her way, in the sense that she waited fifteen minutes at the supermarket deli counter. The "point", however, was blunted in that he didn't know she had waited. The purpose of the move was for her own feeling of superiority, superior martyrdom in the modern sense of martyrdom, which would not even insubstantially advance her position against *White*.

10. "What kind of a tuna?"
10. "Albacore. In water. The only kind we buy."

Larkin treated this needless question by adopting the voice reserved after she misplaced the car keys.

11. "I mean: Chunk or Solid White."
11. "Why does *that* matter?"

12. Since he started eating tuna salad with mayonnaise.

Yes, he had learned something during the "His or Her Freedom" game when he objected to the condiment being added to the tuna. Whether Cynthia's response is a truthful reflection or a lie, it dismisses the fact of someone changing a predilection or behavior. The commentator cannot refrain from reflecting on the nature of change in individuals who are in a long-lasting relationship. While both spouses desire that their partner change many disagreeable opinions, habits, and attributes, when changes alter behavior, their respective response to change is closer to resentment rather than relief. Why resentment? It would be psychologically cheap to explain the response as envy over being able to change. More likely, one has grown accustomed to the aggravating behaviors and any change is annoying because it means one must adjust to the change. Cynthia's upcoming responses (**12 & 13**) embody an inability to adjust or even to admit that she has adjusted, which would indirectly compliment Pillsbury on his ability to change, a move she would not have made many years before.

12. (*Black*) "I thought you always used mayonnaise."

13. (*White*) He had always despised mayonnaise. He had occasion years ago to send back a hoagie made at a deli for using mayo instead of oil.
13. (*Black*) "It's in potato salad and cole slaw, the sauce we use for crab claws, mixed with Dijon mustard."

Dijon vous, she thought, figuring this wasn't the time to express a witticism aloud.

14. (*White*) "I've used mayo in tuna salad for several years."
14. (*Black*) "Okay, okay."

15. (*White*) "Don't 'Okay, okay' me. Obviously, it hasn't made a deep enough impression why I. . . ."

When the elements of a discussion become self-conscious to both interlocutors, the ground is being readied about the thing being elaborated on. The encroaching loathing for the other player becomes inevitable, ultimately destabilizing their respective strategies. In this instance, the players had consciously avoided scratching their spouse's feelings. Larkin's last try to restrain her emotional antagonism is manifested by her next move, which collapses with the addition of "now" to her question.

15. (*Black*) She unscrews the mayonnaise lid as he finishes opening the can of tuna. He drains the water from the tuna can. "What's wrong now, Bill?"

16. (*White*) "What brand is that? It's not Hellman's."
16. (*Black*) "I used it last week when I made you a sandwich."

17. (*White*) He hadn't seen her make it.
17. (*Black*) "You didn't notice when you ate it."

18. (*White*) "Obviously. But I see you using it now."
18. (*Black*) "What's the difference?"

19. (*White*) "A big difference. I know I don't like that brand."
19. (*Black*) "It's all in your mind."

White's observation seems to put some finality to their issue over mayonnaise. This is to say, regardless what happens next, she has told him in so many words that it doesn't really matter to her anymore, that she has little heart to continue the game, which in itself should have given her a distinct advantage. Instead, there was parrying with rubber epees; making the contact with their emotional bodies decidedly unfelt.

20. (*White*) "I don't suppose we have onion and celery."
20. (*Black*) "I'm putting shallots in mine."

Bill still didn't know whether there were any onions. He had to waste a move.

21. (*White*) Finds a large shallot beneath a bag of carrots.
21. (*Black*) She finished her sandwich before he had made the salad.

22. (*White*) "Are you making the kids anything?"
22. (*Black*) "Give Emily some of your salad."

23. (*White*) "She doesn't like mayonnaise."

He was going to eat all of it, having salvaged less than a quarter of the tomato.

23. (*Black*) "She doesn't like lunch meat, either."

24. (*White*) "Why did you tell her they killed cows to get

meat?."

24. (*Black*) "She asked. I don't like to lie to her."

25. (*White*) "She doesn't seem worried when we eat meat."
25. (*Black*) Cynthia went to the nearest pizza place and got a slice for Emily and herself, eating her slice at the shop.

26. (*White*) Bill went out later for a slice himself.

Draw.

Repetitive moves will stop any game. Not long after this subterranean epic confrontation, moves toward divorce were initiated – mutually.

MATCH SCORE Pillsbury 5 – 4 – 6 – 1
                       Larkin 4 – 5 – 6 – 1

MATCH SUMMARY VII

Game 18

The Children Game

Every game in this Match includes some moves from other games. None more so than the 18th game. Yet these same moves take different if not opposite meanings. Woe to anyone expecting an absolute reality or a rose is a rose is a rose. Emily and Tara initially had parental champions, not that the parents would admit it. Likewise, one would expect an overreaction from the girls as they would expect equal affection from their parents. Worse were the times when both parents favored one child over the other. (Not an issue in this match, but Bill often thought, between the ages of 8 and 10, that his older sister was favored because she was a prize student in elementary school and he, the poster boy for mediocrity.) Before Emily came into this world, Cynthia controlled affection for the child. 3. **To be named after the poet...well, every student in Cynthia's English classes could have told you what the name of her daughter-to-be would be!** The name itself pushed Bill away but he didn't resent it. Seemed very natural, and his family and friends concurred with his feeling. Although, this may have been the result of his having said 1...**"Do you think you're pregnant?"** to start the game. Tara had no greater champion than her dad, who was much happier with Cynthia's second pregnancy. Cynthia's strength early in the game centered on performing the thankless duty of taking Emily and, then, Emily and Tara, to Church on Sundays and most holy days. The girls squirmed in the pews, touched other congregants' purses and clothing, talked and laughed. Cynthia suffered the sour looks of fellow worshipers around her, even catching scowls from the priests celebrating the Masses. Not once did the girls ask why Daddy wasn't there. Never were the children more relieved than when, on a weekend in Dad's company, there wasn't the faintest mention of going to church. The children's subsequent attachment to either parent proceeded logically. Neither Cynthia nor Bill consciously treated them differently – no good cop - bad cop – but somehow the kids knew. Playing favorites might not be an animal thing. What Mom and Dad allowed for each girl was filed away for the moment, and ten or twenty years hence a move would result: **36...Both girls preferred to stay with Bill and his new wife for the Thanksgiving holiday.** And while the move looks decisive and marks a path for a potential victory for Dad, just by knocking an unsuspecting Mom off balance, one might be surprised by her response: **37. Cynthia used the free time to take a six-day holiday and fly to London, where she saw many plays and took excursions to Stratford-on-Avon, Oxford and Cambridge, and Stonehenge.** Also, by this time, Emily was attending college: **32. Cynthia's eldest daughter decided to major in Accounting** and, earlier, **22. Emily didn't read many books except those assigned at school.**

Tara, meanwhile, has spent much time with Bill who **26... took her on hiking trips in the Poconos and Adirondacks.** When the kids emulated their parents' habits, usually the bad ones, Bill and Cynthia occasionally used these for some imagined advantage. **12. "I heard Emily curse the other day," said Cynthia, "one of your timeless epithets." 12..."I heard her, and I wouldn't consider 'doggone it' a form of cursing." 13. "She's only five years old."** Bill must've remembered this exchange. **18..."Emily called Tara a little dick," Bill said, smiling. 19. 'Tara was being mean to her." 19..."She hears you call me that!" 20. "I call you a big dick. Besides, at least she didn't call her a little cunt."** Ultimately, the game stalled over many years, as the decisive bad move was not taken by either parent via the kids. Namely, the couple remained friendly, that is, avoided a deadly break through a misunderstanding or kept from acting like ignorant, selfish assholes.

MATCH SCORE Pillsbury 5 – 4 – 7 – 1
                     Larkin 4 – 5 – 7 – 1

The Vocation Game

While Pillsbury's future looked good after Game 4, it belied his real insecurities as a player. Larkin could not have had a better game. Also, this game continued the bad trend for the white pieces.

Pillsbury *White* Larkin *Black*

1. (*White*) "When are the teachers at your school going to form a union?"

1. (*Black*) "What's a seven-letter word for a garden with bushes in the shape of animals?"

2. (*White*) "Public Schools pay thirty to fifty percent more than hers for someone with her experience."

The kind of move ostensibly shows deference if not respect for the opponent while it really says that *Black* will be foolish to continue at her school. Further, *Black* should know that *White* is fully aware that she wouldn't trade her job for one at a public or any other type of school. *Black*'s best response is to play the game she's most comfortable playing.

2. (*Black*) "You'd think a landscaper would know something like that."

3. (*White*) She could get a better IRA plan.

3. (*Black*) "The fourth letter's an 'i' and the last is a 'y.'"

4. (*White*) "Why don't you ever check the puzzle answers the next week?"

Her will to remain on the crossword until he got off the subject of her job and future had worked. She had several similar moves in the wings. Further, *White* left her with an opening.

4. (*Black*) "That's why you'll never understand the pleasure one gets from doing one."

5. (*White*) Bill did the *TV Guide* crosswords in high school.

5. (*Black*) "You'd think you'd know the answer to a football question."

Just as good: **5...**"**They were too easy**" or "**Were they the ones that had the celebrity photo in the center?**" *Black* opted to disdain mentioning a form of crossword beneath the dignity of the semi-literate.

6. (*White*) "Teachers don't know much about the real world, not having to worry about making a profit or losing business," Bill opined at one of Cynthia's Christmas parties.

6. (*Black*)*"They're easy for you because you were an English*

major in college."

Black wants *White* to think that she will let the comment pass. Also, a return to the kind of moves replete in Game Three shows that she entered this game with strong plans for attack and defense. The latter is reflected in the way she's established her position re: the crosswords. Her use of a game within a game, in fact, outruns *Black*'s attempts to establish a willful male attitude in Game One with the fantasy football moves. Black also thwarts *White*'s attempt to steer the game back in direction of the "union" and "IRA" moves.

7. (*White*) Bill worked several summers at the shore as a hotel desk clerk, and his first job in eighth grade was caddying.
7. (*Black*) *"I worked my way through college."*

8. (*White*) "I didn't have the luxury of majoring in something that wasn't going to help me get a job later."(?)

White's response was exactly what *Black* was hoping for. Reflexive and strategically chaotic. Better for *White*: **8. "I partied all through college,"** which, while seeming to contradict the statement *Black* had used against *White*, was very true. He had gone to a branch campus of a state university for two years and when he transferred to the main campus he let his inhibitions down. Followed by **9.**

Bill had a 3.2 cumulative average. The only worse move would have been **8. I majored in Business Administration.**

8. (*Black*) "Bill had more jobs than girlfriends before he met me," she often said to her friends.

9. (*White*) *"He does WHAT for a living?" her mother supposedly cried out when Cynthia told her. "Thank God your father isn't alive."*

Possibly too late to invoke that particular bit of Cynthiania. First, he didn't believe Mrs Larkin had said that. Second, she hadn't told him this directly. He had heard it fourth hand as it made the rounds from her to their friends. Third, Bill harbored a private pleasure in giving her mother psychological grief.

9. (*Black*) She always wanted to be an English teacher.

10. (*White*) "I don't have to go back to school."
10. (*Black*) "He cuts grass for a living," Mrs Larkin tells her friends.

11. (*White*) His boss at the landscaping business promised that Bill could own half the franchise in a few years.
11. (*Black*) "You feel like you're building future generations when you are a teacher; the money means very little."

12. (*White*) Bill always feels he must earn more than he's earning at a given time to provide for his family.

12. (*Black*) Cynthia emphasizes that they are in this together. Don't the bills get paid every month?

13. (*White*) Children to support. A house and two cars. Insurance for everything. Retirement considerations. Vacations. They can never be complacent.(?)

Worrying in place of moves! *White* believes that he alone is responsible for the work-sustenance dynamic. His weak play in this game, that is, his apparent lack of a unified strategy, directly reflects his playing as if his opponent were absent. While this lack of strategy might have been appropriate for pre-20th century Grand Masters, the archaic mindset of *White* ruined his usual withering aggressive mentality.

13. (*Black*) Cynthia's relatives often suggest to Bill that he ought to go into the real estate business.

14. (*White*) "You're always complaining about your job."

14. (*Black*) *Dear Ms. Larkin, ...my daughter could not have plagiarized because there are no such thing as original ideas, that is, all ideas have to be derived from someone or somewhere....*

If there were a move that said "fuck it all" with teaching,

this was it. Fortunately, Larkin didn't face this nonsense very often. It just seemed so because of the contempt in her voice when she spoke about it. Giving Bill the wrong idea about how she really felt was actually all Bill's doing as he groped for any straw that could bring her choice of profession into doubt.

15. (*White*) Bill starts a landscaping business with his friend, Tom Gentry.
15. (*Black*) Cynthia tells Sue King that Tommy spends more time at the track than around the business, to which Sue replies that the guy must be a bachelor or have been divorced.

16. (*White*) "I don't know when I wrote a paper that I didn't plagiarize," Bill tells Tom.
16. (*Black*) "I staked him to the tune of ten thousand from my trust fund," she tells Sue.

17. (*White*) Bill agrees with the mother, Mrs. Akers, that the student's research paper didn't exactly copy from the movie review and that the coincidence of the two opinions had seemed plausible.
17. (*Black*) She complains to Sue about not getting support from her own husband. Bad enough her principal cut her off at the knees.

Straying from commenting on the game, the commentator

believes there is a strange rule in this culture. It involves expecting others to help; it is a culture of cultivating dependency and therefore of abuse of privacy. The circle of friends generates its own unhappiness through its members' willing acceptance of personal weakness.

18. (*White*) "She brought in an expert on plagiarism and the kids just got more confused," he tells Tom.

The continued weakness of Pillsbury's moves emerge from the shameless position he has taken toward the plagiarism case. Kathleen Akers wrote a critical view of a movie and had apparently been influenced by Roger Ebert's syndicated column in the *Trenton Times*. Bill would have been better off with **19. Why did the kid write about a movie that sucked so much?** because, despite the crudeness of the opinion, it would have avoided the artificial position of agreeing with the parent. He could have followed up with **20. The mother's a bigger asshole than the kid.** Pillsbury was aware that during the conference between Cynthia and Mrs. Akers, the plagiarist was present and acted smugly and spoke sarcastically to Cynthia about the mother's apparent approval.

18. (*Black*) Sue tells her friend, Judy, about Bill not getting his own franchise and having to go into debt to start a business, and that Cynthia thought Bill would be bankrupt in six months.

19. (*White*) His busiest time of year was when she had her vacation.

19. (*Black*) Takes summer courses for a Masters in secondary school administration.

20. (*White*) Bill looks at the Community College Adult Classes catalog and finds several Real Estate courses.

20. (*Black*) Cynthia tells Sue that Bill's making a good career move by going into Real Estate.

This move counters a potential move from Pillsbury later in the game: **Is your husband still cutting lawns for a living?** Regardless of the move's consequences, all players would have to marvel at Pillsbury's courage for such a self-deprecating display. Yet, it would be effective for many reasons. One, his career choice affects her standing in society and gives an implicit strength or weakness to her game, depending. On what? Whether or not his landscaping job will be perceived pejoratively: for example, **how could children respect a father who mows lawns for a living?** or worse: **how could she marry a college graduate who mows lawns?**, or perceived positively: **her salary's nearly a third higher than her husband's** or **she must make the most of the economic decisions in that household**. On the other hand, he rarely benefits from Larkin working as a teacher because few people really respect the teaching profession below the university level. If she were an accountant or a business executive he would have benefited in the game more that she would have.

21. (*White*) The business loses money in proportion to Tommy's visit to the racetracks.
21. (*Black*) She complains to him that they can't take a vacation at the shore.

22. (*White*) "We can stay a week."
22. (*Black*) "Who wants to rent for a week? We'll hardly be unpacked before we'll be ready to leave. Emily will just be getting to know some of the children on the beach when she'll have to go."

Pillsbury suffers many problems with this weak move. First, it fails worse than did Chamberlain at Munich as an attempt at appeasement. Second, he allowed his opponent to get at least three moves into one. Third, she used his child against him in one of these moves within the move. Lastly, the question of the vacation, brought up by Larkin in **move 22**, diverted him from his business failure initiative; namely, he could have stayed on track with **23. He's thinking of suing the bastard** or even **23. He's my friend, I couldn't sue him** and **24. He'll pay us back fifty dollars a month for the next ten years** or even better **24. Bill has hired a lawyer and put a lien against any of Tommy's future paychecks.** There was even the remote chance had he could follow through with a *coup de grace* in the endgame: **The Pillsburys own Tommy's house!**

23. (White) "You might have to put your Masters on hold."

It advances Pillsbury's game by preserving some vestige of his ego. Just as Philip II of Spain thought it better to lose the battle of the Spanish Armada than never sending the fleet at all, because he had known more than a year before he sent the fleet that it was an impossible operation with no hope for success, Bill could live with a lower income rather than see his wife receive a degree that would have pushed her career above the cloying everyday procedures of teaching. As mentioned in Game one's commentary, the logic underpinning much of his strategy, of keeping her happy did not necessarily mean that she should be happy outside their marriage relationship. For Larkin, though, making him happy is part of her defensive strategy by maintaining the (societal) illusion of inherent male superiority. Are all marriage games like this or just most of them?

23. (*Black*) "I'm pregnant," she tells him at dinner.

24. (*White*) Bill tells Tom how having a second kid now really screws things up financially, but he's never been happier.
24. (*Black*) "How can you still talk to that guy?"

25. (*White*) "Don't tell anyone, especially your mother," he says to Cynthia after failing the Real Estate test.

25. (*Black*) "He wasn't ready to take it, Mom. And don't ever bring it up in front of him."

26. (*White*) Hired by another landscaping company.

Taking the Real Estate test was not his mistake, nor was failing it. The aftermath killed him. **26. "Don't tell anybody...."** in combination with **27. Hired by another....** were feeble attempts to save face. Not that we're saying **26. "Lets go over to your mother's to celebrate"** would have fooled anyone. It was too late for **Took the Real Esate test without telling anyone** because he had committed himself publicly to taking the sting away from his entrepreneurial failure. Move **27** was necessary for continuing the game. The fact that he was still speaking to Tommy after the initial problem of the missing funds in the business's bank account, practically assures Larkin a victory.

26. (*Black*) A year after having Tara, Cynthia continues her classes for the Master in administration.

27. (*White*) Passes the Real Estate exam the third time.

27. (*Black*) From Cynthia Larkin's resumé:
1996. Made Headmaster at Moorestown Friends School
1999. Inducted into her college's Academic Hall of Fame
2001. Univ. of Massachusetts Press publishes Cynthia's

Master's thesis: *The Teacher and the Principal: Ways to Achieve High Level Integration and Results from Non-Tracking Curricula*

28. (*White*) From William Pillsbury's resumé:
1996. Assistant Manager of Freelawn Associate Garden Maintenance
1998. Joins Century 21
2000. Joins Remax
2002. Assistant Manager of Chem Lawn franchise in Princeton, NJ.

Why does Bill continue this folly? Were this a match in Japan, seppuku may have been a winning move in this type of game despite its negative ramifications on the match as a whole, especially if the man were to win the match by dying. Where would be the joy in winning? In Japan, perhaps, there would be some consolation. That is, the man would know that the woman would not publicly, at least, have expressed any claims to have won the match by default. Remember too in America having an inferior job has the consolation -- oh if this were only true for Bill -- of making more money. This might have been the case had Bill stuck with Real Estate.

28. (*Black*) Fired a teacher at the Friends school for protesting the school's drive to supply basic needs, like toothbrushes and Dentyne, earmarked for a village in

Iraq destroyed by American warplanes.

29. (*White*) After working two months for Remax, he sold his first house.

29. (*Black*) Receives a phone message from Bill's office that there was a fire two days before settlement.

30. (*White*) RESIGNS

The feeling that he would never surpass her clung to Bill the entire game. He could never convince himself that Cynthia didn't revel in his inferiority, and never told her he went back to the landscaping business where, he finally admitted to himself, he was the happiest working. Had he said "fuck it all" regarding college and all schooling his game may have improved with his possessing a clearer head and he might have met Cynthia on an equal plane.

MATCH SCORE Pillsbury 5 – 5 – 7 – 1
                   Larkin 5 – 5 – 7 – 1

Game 20 (1980-2004)

Past Lovers Game

A game unrivaled for twists and made opportunities. Continually appearing as if neither or both could win. Its end has an unpredictable predictability when both players seek mutual annihilation.

Larkin: *White*   Pillsbury: *Black*

1. (*White*) "You didn't really love Gena, did you?"

If a first move could capture a piece, this would be it.

1. (*Black*) "She wants me to say I never loved her," Bill had told many of his friends over the years.

2. (*White*) "He never had real closure with his first love," she tells Clara, her best friend.

2. (*Black*) He often asks whether her last ex, Demetrius, "the Greek," got a green card or remained an illegal alien.

3. (*White*) Told her girlfriends that Demetrius was chauvinistic but Greek men knew how to "treat" a woman.

3. (*Black*) He never forgot Gena, his first girlfriend, whom he dated freshman year at college; not only they never go to bed, they never even French-kissed.

4. (*White*) "You must have hated the Virgin deep down."
(?)

A weakness of *White*'s Game: an early attack before her own defenses were prepared. Her moves against *Black*'s memory of previous girlfriends may indeed have been justified, but this tactic might have realized a greater strategic value late in this game when it will have been necessary to reduce absolutely *Black*'s idyllic years to mush.

4. (*Black*) Gena became a born-again Christian and told Bill it was either Christ or him.

5. (*White*) *He didn't want sex with her. Just to be near her always.*

White comes back from a poor move with a very innovative plan, albeit one easy to copy by her opponent; namely, make a countermove move with your opponent's words from conversations, primarily intimate and personal.

5. (*Black*) Bill believed himself capable of non-sexual love and had meant his wife to interpret that he could feel the same for her.

White saw the move as a naked statement of his undying affection for the Virgin and that he could *only* have strong love for a woman that he had never fucked. Better for Pillsbury: **5. . . . It was his real experience of love.** At least this avoids assaulting *White* with her own words.

6. (*White*) "Did you keep a picture of her?"
6. (*Black*) *Her first sexual experience was with Danny Meltzer in a motel. She thought she would marry him. Danny eventually owned his own gas station.*

She should've ended the gambit with **6. "Get over her!"**.

7. (*White*) She dreams often about Demetrius.
7. (*Black*) "Didn't you say Demetrius didn't like kids?"

8. (*White*) "Did you ever get over *any* of your old girlfriends?"

Too late a move amid moves made too early.

8. (*Black*) He had met Alisandra in his junior at college at a party in his apartment building.

9. (*White*) Demetrius had followed Cynthia back to the United States from Crete.
9. (*Black*) Alisandra's goal in life was to work as a reporter for WABC television in New York.

10. (*White*) *Alisandra didn't think he'd ever be well-connected*

enough to land her a broadcasting job.
10. (Black) Demetrius said she was his only love; she never trusted him.

11. (*White*) Cynthia found Demetrius a job in West Orange as a newspaper delivery driver.

An attempt to develop a line of play whereby she could support the men she lived with. In a potential Match with Demetrius, Larkin would have gained a considerable advantage and nearly made "the Greek" cherish his defeats. Understanding *Black*'s sensitivities, she alluded to her stable job versus Bill's unsatisfactory position at the landscaping firm. **11. "Bill drives a lawn mower for a living"** would have been too cruel a play; moreover, the previous game was less about Pillsbury's manhood as related to work than his physical prowess with women.

11. (*Black*) He had screwed Alisandra more times than he had all his other woman before, during, and after he was married. Although he never mentioned this to Cynthia, he thought she suspected as much.

12. (White)"You never mentioned to your parents you were living with 'the Greek'."
12. (Black) "They would have never found out if you hadn't blabbed it at Thanksgiving."

13. (*White*)*"It was Christmas."*
13. (*Black*) *"Fuck you."*

14. (*White*) *Alisandra dumped him after he graduated from Fordham. She had two more years to go and she fell in love with a journalism professor.*
14. (*Black*) *Demetrius wanted to go back to his home island, Chios, to start a restaurant.*

15. (*White*) *He telephoned the Virgin when he got the break-up letter from Alisandra.*
15. (*Black*) *Demetrius hit her once. (!)*

16. (*White*) *Gena asked him to go to a prayer meeting.*

There are fewer moves left in this game at such an early juncture than in any other game in recent history. *Black's* slight but decisive early advantage is being pressed on every exchange.

16. (*Black*) "It was a Christian social club. Guitars and singing and testimonials. During Christmas vacation."

17. (*White*) And you still went!
17. (*Black*) The master of ceremonies went to different tables asking what Christmas meant to certain individuals. He put the mike up to Bill's face. Gena looked at him, waiting for who knows what. He said "Christmas' meant

nothing to him."

18. (White) *They gave me a standing ovation.*
18. (*Black*) *"You wouldn't hit me, Bill?"*

Larkin had asked this after he had given her the engagement ring. Pillsbury using this indicates that he's determined to come out of the Match a winner.

19. (White) *He became a dedicated non-Christian from then on.*
19. (Black) Bill dated three women after Alisandra over the next year; two divorcees with children, and a college dropout druggie.

20. (*White*) He screwed everything in sight, she thought many times – and may have said this aloud more than once.   (?)

While not an untrue move, her thinking becomes questionable because she believes she's quoting her husband; however, *Black* was never so foolish to confide his adventures to anyone but one male friend. Cynthia's assumption caused an automatic click of alienation within Bill if for no other reason than that she was one of several women he was screwing when he was screwing her.

20. (*Black*) Bill picked up many women at bars, one of

whom was Carole, a friend of Cynthia's, but before he knew Cynthia. He felt no compunction to inform Cynthia, it was a one-night stand.

21. (*White*) *What about your own unresolved relationship with David Wellsley?*
21. (*Black*) He never mentioned his liason with a 50-year old woman on a cruise to the Bahamas.

22. (*White*) "David called me the other day," Carole told Cynthia, "he was wondering where you were. Did you ever tell him you got married?"
22. (*Black*) Carole told Bill that she didn't want her husband, Joe, who was the jealous type, to know about their fling.

A defensive move that appears strong at first but could create a vulnerable position in the endgame.

23. (*White*) "Was he upset when you told him I was...?" "I didn't tell him," Carole replied. Keeping options available....
23. (*Black*) After the *Star Wars* video collection was advertised on television, Bill recalls the time in 1981 when he saw *The Empire Strikes Back* with Gena.

24. (*White*) David had taken Cynthia to *The Big Chill*.
24. (*Black*) "Did David ever say he would marry you?"

Interesting parry. Black recalls the mistake from Game One move **2. "I always figured we'd get married"** and tries to apply this lesson from history.

25. (*White*) "Only when I got a divorce from you."

So much for history. A nice response for a couple reasons. First, *Black* does not know that David is still in the dark about Cynthia. This move will only lose its force should Bill stumble upon the truth, which is unlikely. Second, it introduces a flourish lacking from *White*'s previous moves. She shows a weapon that he didn't think she would use. Divorce. *Black* can take pause: *White* has another potential if not better player in the wings with whom to match her psyche.

25. (*Black*) "His wife dead yet?"

So much for Bill's ignorance. He knew one or two strategic facts about David. The son of a bitch was married when Cynthia went with him. The wife was an invalid who, to make matters worse, knew and approved of her husband's affair with the "chippy."

26. (*White*) "Is there ever anything you're afraid to tell me?"

Nice change of pace. Neatly echoes a motif in the game.

Notice she wasn't asking *Black* to reveal secrets. She wants to probe the inherent honesty and deception in their marriage. A move one can make to distract an opponent or to engage him at the most elemental level. Usually seen at this part of a match as a distraction; in endgame, it is deadly serious.

26. (*Black*) He assumed he would never want to know let alone learn what was on his wife's mind at any particular moment.

27. (*White*) "Do you still love her?"
27. (*Black*) "Of course not."

27... **"Who?"** would have been indefensible. He *had to assume* she was speaking about Alisandra. To think she had remotely referred to The Virgin would have revealed that she was still on *Black*'s mind and, consequently, he had never gotten over the relationship.

29. (*White*) After giving birth to her second daughter, she wonders whether David's a widower.
29. (Black) Bill briefly gets together with Carole during his wife's second pregnancy.

A repugnant move. Surely none of *White*'s supporters could appreciate its value toward winning this game. Is it enough for *White*'s handlers to ask rhetorically whether winning is worth a move like *Black*'s **29**: wondering if she and David could pick up where they had left off? In fact, the move came less from desire than from inertia. Unworthy of a (!) because he both felt guilty and safe with this relationship.

30. (*White*) Why was Bill doing the wash as soon as he came home from work?
30. (*Black*) He explained that his shirt and jeans were sweaty from a job that afternoon.

31. (White) Other clothes were on the floor. Why didn't he throw them into the wash with his sweaty ones?
31. (Black) He didn't know whether the colors would bleed.

32. (*White*) It was only three o'clock in the afternoon. He usually got home around six or seven during the summer months.
32. (*Black*) "We let the work crew off at 2:30. The truck was low on gasoline."

33. (*White*) Bill shouldn't be washing the shirt except on the permanent press cycle.
33. (*Black*) Did it matter?

34. (*White*) Wasn't it strange that he had a towel in the wash with his pants, shirt and underwear?

34. (*Black*) He had thrown the towel into the washer the night before.

35. (*White*) "You're sure he's not cheating on you?" Cynthia's mother responds after hearing her daughter mention Bill's odd behavior.

Excruciating pressure on *Black* makes **32. . . "let the work crew off early. . . ."** a brilliant play. Because all of White's moves from **30.** and after are a screen for the tremendous defense in Black's next move.

35. (*Black*) "Cynthia, all men are cheating, lousy liars," says Mrs. Larkin. "Some day you'll catch him in a lie. Pull on that lie and it will be attached to his cheating."

For everyone's sake, it was good *White*'s mother continued talking and relieved *Black* of making the move he was saving for a more desperate situation than this game allowed: **37. Three years ago Mrs. Larkin had accused Bill of making love to her the night before her daughter married him.** The force of genetics has hurt Larkin in this game. Cynthia might think her mother paranoid and delusional. It is difficult to forget that Mrs Larkin might have put the family pet in the oven after it had died believing the warmth would revive it. In the back reservoir of Cynthia's mind, a similar voice speaks to her in what, analogously, is a foreign language.

36. (*White*) Most men she had known intimately, especially, Demetrius, would listen sympathetically to her whenever she was depressed.   (?)

An uncertain move, half-admitting that a guy could get into her panties by feigning attention to her problems.

36. (*Black*) She had forgotten that she had once called Bill a good listener.

37. (*White*) "I'd like to go back to Malta some day."
37. (*Black*) Bill had never been overseas.

38. (*White*) She remembered a particular beach, black sand, alone with Demetrius, naked.

Although it did not affect the quality of the move, Larkin was actually on the Greek island of Santorini at the time.

38. (*Black*) He went on a cruise to Bermuda and remembered little about the island, except a beach with pink sand.

39. (*White*) She remembered the great time in Malta after having watched a movie, that was filmed there, late one Saturday evening. She had missed the beginning and had not seen the title. It had starred some guy and, she thinks, the woman who played Lois Lane in the Christopher

Reeve's *Superman.*

39. (*Black*) "Gena and I went to *Superman 3*," he said.

40. (*White*) Cynthia, who wasn't watching the game but reading a novel by Joyce Carol Oates, commented that she didn't like the *Superman* movies..

White knows the next move of her opponent and knows her move to counter that move! How many times did they have to play the same game? She would know had she read Nietzsche!!

40. (Black) "I always thought Gena resembled Margot Kidder."

41. (White) Demetrius resembled Tom Conti.

On the surface a brilliant play. Conti had yet played the role of the Greek in *Shirley Valentine*. She was thinking of him in *Reuben, Reuben*. Unfortunately, despite getting an Academy Award nomination, his name generates little fear in *Black*. *White* never realized this, for all the times she played the move.

41. (Black) "After we broke up, there was a call at my house, about seven months later, my father answered, I wasn't home, and he asked who was calling and the girl replied 'Margot'."

And *White* regrets she didn't use something similar to *Black's* move **41** with David or Demetrius, a move every bit as vicious as the boomerang thrown in *The Road Warrior: Beyond the Thunderdome.*

42. (*White*) *Demetrius didn't like women challenging him, otherwise he wouldn't have treated his girlfriends like dirt.*

You can tell that the Endgame has started.

42. (*Black*) *Alisandra even said that he had never gotten over the Virgin, and this was the real reason Alisandra broke off the relationship.*

Smart. Again making a play that Cynthia would have liked to have done sooner or later.

43. (*White*) The Virgin's a good example. She was looking for Jesus or God to be subservient to. "Bill was never more pleased by this competition," she often told her friends.
43. (*Black*) Gena called him three years after he had graduated from college to tell him that she was married and pregnant.

44. (*White*) "Didn't Alisandra do that to you as well?"

Fine comeback. Leveling the number of pieces on each side even. *White* revealed a character defect in *Black*, one hard to pinpoint, like a recessive gene that ultimately issues its biological verdict; namely, Bill had done something unspeakably wrong to these women such that they had been compelled to strike back at him many years later.

44. (Black) "Didn't Demetrius stay in the States hoping you'd get a divorce in a year or two?" Bill asked Cynthia the day they had signed the divorce papers.

45. (*White*) "I understand The Virgin's left her husband," she replied. "So much for Ms Christianity."
45. (*Black*) A woman answers the phone at Bill's house four months after the divorce. Cynthia hangs up.

46. (*White*) Cynthia drives by Bill's house in the evenings three or four times to see whether she can see anyone in the lighted rooms.

The game, the Match, is slipping away. *Black* shows no concern for his opponent's potential relationships during the critical year after the divorce.

46. (*Black*) After a meeting with Emily's teachers, two years later, Bill tells Cynthia about his engagement to Regina Pettyjohn.

47. (*White*) "I'm seeing one of the. . . ."

White RESIGNS in the middle of her statement.

Stopping in mid-sentence, she discerned the NAME within the formal disguise. Regina - Gena. The Virgin. All *White* had left, to avoid Mate, was the perfunctory 47. **When did she get divorced?** and 48. **When did you hook up with her?** The latter question, especially, she did not want the answer to.

MATCH SCORE Pillsbury 6 – 5 - 7 – 1
                   Larkin 5 – 6 – 7 – 1

WINNER   William Pillsbury

After attending Columbia University School of the Arts for a brief time, Robert Castle traveled around Europe and lived on and off in Florence, Italy. He taught American History, Film Criticism, and Sociology at a small academy outside Trenton, NJ. His most recent published novel was *The Hidden Life* (Atmosphere Press, 2020). In 2006 he had three books published *A Sardine on Vacation* (fiction, Spuyten Duyvil, 2006), *The End of a Travel* (Memoir, Ravenna Press) and *Odd Pursuits* (short stories, Wild Child Press). Since 2000, he has published over 50 articles in *Bright Lights Film Journal* and over 160 other pieces on movies. Since 2005, he has written many plays, some performed in NYC, Great Britain, and Philadelphia. He is married and has no children.

www.ingramcontent.com/pod-product-compliance
Lightning Source LLC
Chambersburg PA
CBHW031051310726
48969CB00007B/2216